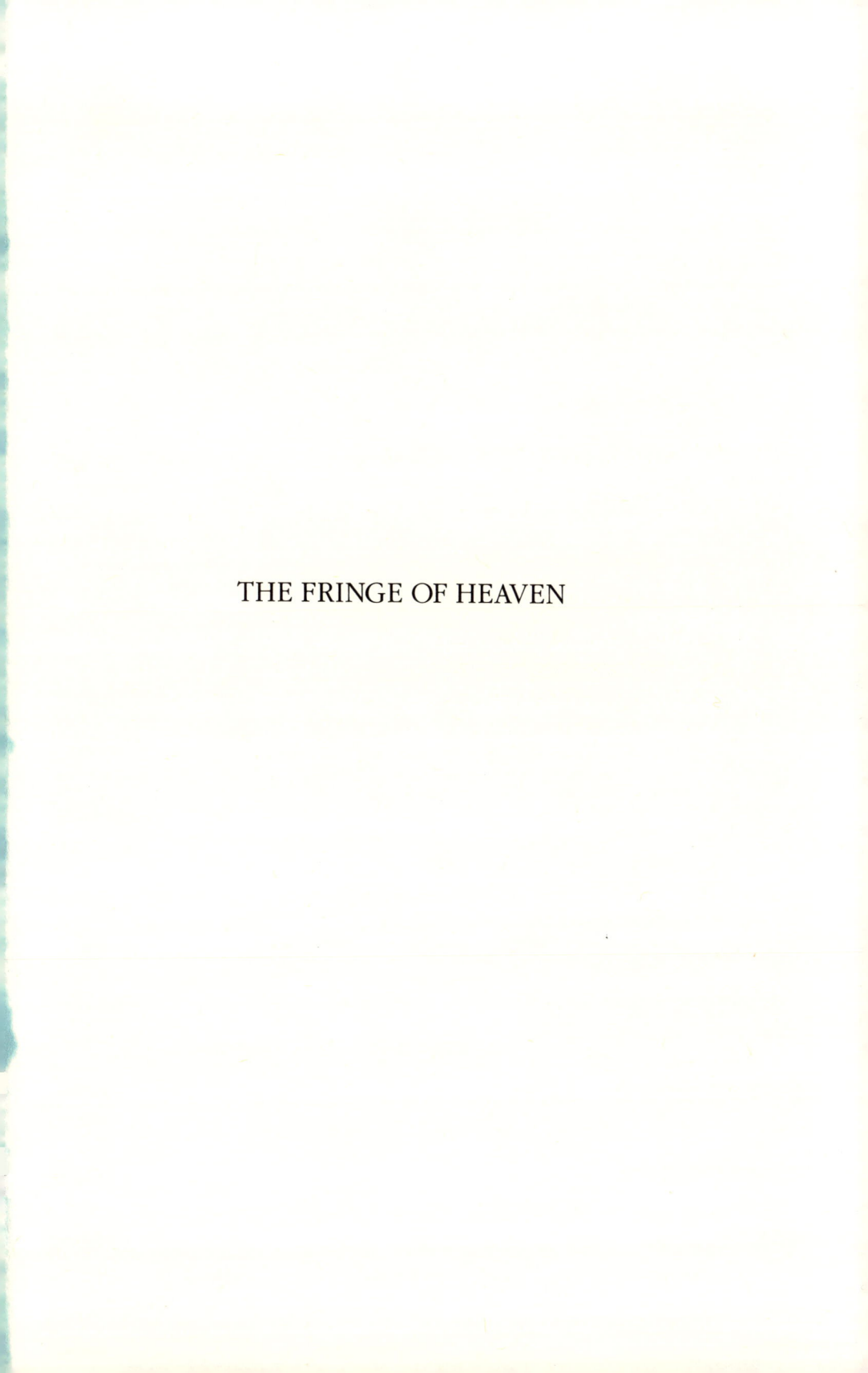

THE FRINGE OF HEAVEN

Also by Margaret Sutherland

DARK PLACES, DEEP REGIONS
and Other Stories

Margaret Sutherland

THE FRINGE OF HEAVEN

A Novel

Stemmer House
PUBLISHERS, INC.

OWINGS MILLS, MARYLAND

Copyright © 1984 by Margaret Sutherland

All rights reserved

No part of this book may be used or reproduced in any form or in any manner whatsoever, electrical or mechanical, including xerography, microfilm, recording and photocopying, without written permission, except in the case of brief quotations in critical articles and reviews.

Inquiries should be directed to
Stemmer House Publishers, Inc.
2627 Caves Road
Owings Mills, Maryland, 21117

A Barbara Holdridge book
Printed and bound in the United States of America
First Edition

Library of Congress Cataloging in Publication Data

Sutherland, Margaret.
  The fringe of heaven.

  "A Barbara Holdridge book."
  I. Title.
PR9639.3.S95F7   1984   823   84-8528
ISBN 0-88045-044-4

For their hospitality during the term of my fellowship
I wish to thank the staff of the English Department
at Auckland University.

I also thank Marcus Campbell for his considerable
assistance with editing; and Sulfiati Walsh
for background information.

For our all-weather friends
Hassan and Felena Sills

The passage quoted in chapter 10 is taken from
Dans le Labyrinthe by Alain Robbe-Grillet.

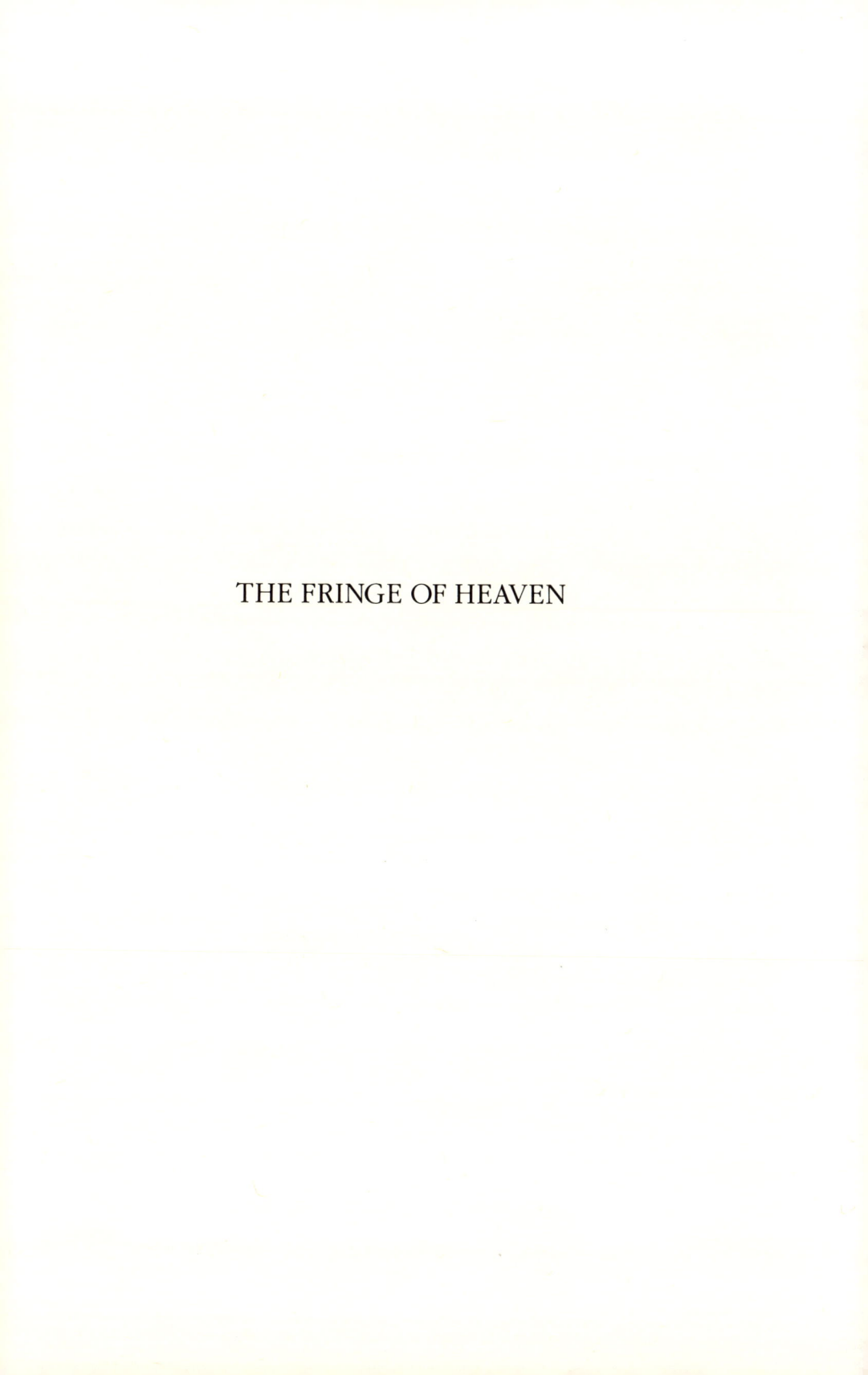

THE FRINGE OF HEAVEN

ONE

There's a stranger in the street.

It's Paul, looking for somewhere to live. He has a flat on the other side of town, but he doesn't care to live there since Linda left and the pot-plants died.

Paul wants Twenty-five. The letter-boxes are secretive. Fourteen is nailed on a lancewood and Sixteen is veiled in jasmine. Eighteen isn't there at all. Paul crosses over.

On the porch of Twenty-three a man is sitting on a stool. He wears a pink plastic cape and he stares straight ahead. His wife is cutting his hair. She must be his wife— she handles him that way. Looking serious, she combs down his hair from the bald crown. She snips, sunlight flashing from the scissors. Wisps of grey fall down. She touches the man's shoulder. He swivels to the right and stares ahead.

Paul rounds the corner. Over the road a caravan grows in long grass. A chaotic little dog whirls out of the caravan. Paul offers his hand and summons a courageous odour. He has heard that dogs bite fear. His sandshoes slither on the banked-up metal. He can smell dust. The sun beats down. The wild ginger's buzzing. Honey perfume drifts.

Paul, who dreams of towers, sees a tower. The house whose tower it is perches at the top of a slope. One day it might slip. For now it considers, like a child at the top of a slide. It's an ordinary house, not out to impress. The tower's not the brick-and-mortar kind built for storybook princesses. Just a six-sided room, it's painted primer-pink like the rest of the additions.

The letter-box has collapsed beside its rotting post. There's only a wooden crate and a stone. Paul can't be sure it's Twenty-five. He takes the uphill track. Paspalum seeds stick to his hands.

At the top of the slope he's puffing, reminded again he's vulnerable. He's getting over hepatitis. Grasping the flaking handrail he rests, then negotiates the rickety steps.

Somewhere he can hear a girl singing, very quietly, very sweetly. He looks through the front door and sees elderly chairs around an oak table and wildflowers in a crystal vase and an easel and cats and cartons of old clothes and, facing the doorway, a gilt-framed oil painting of a beautiful and arrogant young woman. Paul knocks. The canary bursts into song. He knocks again. A door opens and Paul is ambushed by curry aroma. A woman in purple blouse, batik skirt, silver necklace and white ankle socks pauses beneath the younger, gilt-framed Olga.

"I've come about the room," Paul says.

Olga beams. Her plait swings as she ushers him in and settles him down in the one chair with springs. She appraises him with Earl Grey tea from the Georgian teapot, and rather dry herb scones. Paul seems educated and polite—a different kettle of fish from the types who might want cheap board in the distant suburbs.

Paul chews with perseverance on a scone and asks Olga if she does the paintings. Olga sits forward. Her eyes sparkle as she pronounces on creativity versus the pitiable boredom of so many of her neighbours. Eloquently she concludes, "I can't be bothered with boredom," proceeding without pause to Wayang puppets and Samuel Butler, of whom she approves. "Butler rejected all music but Handel's, and all accepted beliefs." She has a gay laugh and strong-looking teeth. She springs to the bookshelves, extracting *Erewhon* for Paul's perusal. He has never examined a first edition, and this is.

"Isn't this valuable?" Respect for money has been instilled into him. Olga just laughs. A bagatelle, her wave implies. As if to tease, she drops *Erewhon* on the table beside the butter-dish. Paul wishes she would put the book away. There are several kittens dashing about and they don't look house-trained. He wonders when Olga will discuss his board and lodging. She seems content with the conversation as it is. Buttering scones, she time-slips from nineteenth-century New Zealand to thirteenth-century France.

"Butler was absolutely right. Be wary of beliefs, they have a way of setting. Take the Catholics and the Cathars. In or out of religion, men love to disagree, it seems to me."

"Who were the Cathars?"

"They said Satan made the world, men are obnoxious. The Church said God made the world, men are good. A minor alteration of perspective, wouldn't you say? Not a bit of it. Count Raymond, one of the so-called pure in heart, was a Cathar. Well, the Pope, with the King's agreement, deposed him and set up a Catholic. Raymond wasn't so pure after all. He had one of his squires assassinate the Papal legate. Naturally enough, the Pope was none too pleased. So away we go on the usual spree; persecution, slaughter. . . ." Olga sinks back and sighs. "Learn from the past, Paul, or else relive it."

A kitten hesitates by the butter. Paul grabs the book and points out the publication date to Olga.

"Look. 1872. You really should take care of this, it can't ever be replaced."

He has forgotten his manners, but Olga smiles as she pats his arm and replaces *Erewhon* on the shelf.

"I think you will be good for me, Paul."

Alas, my love, you do me wrong to cast me off discourteously, sings Rowan in the orchard.

Cross-legged, she sits concealed where moss-covered peach trees bear hard green fruit. Now she regrets coming home from the hospital for her day off. Olga is being difficult. She threatens curry for dinner. On the grounds of the plumber's need, she has tried to borrow the pay cheque earmarked for plum suede boots, a lesser matter of desire. And, regarding Rowan's father, her answers do not satisfy. "We simply drifted." Like rudderless sail boats at the mercy of the wind? Under the peach tree, Rowan sings the last notes of *Greensleeves* and bows to the hydrangeas.

None of it would matter, if she wasn't in love with Jacob, or if Jacob was in love with her. Jacob is the Charge Nurse of the ward where Rowan works. He is both pleasant and kind to her, as he is to all his staff and patients. He paces with manics and sits with those who weep. If he has any peculiarity, no one at the hospital has yet announced it. Jacob is impressive in his work and married.

Rowan sighs and traces the hard peach pressing into her back. She hurls the bullet at the hen coop. The corrugated iron roof rings, and the bantam cock pounds squawking down the slope, careering like a wind-up toy. The cock somehow sums up Olga. He is a gallant bird, a bird of spirit, but he simply doesn't fit in. He has never learned the social order of the run. He won't push in and peck what's due to him. He flaps around the periphery of the brood and has secret places of nourishment. His crow gets on the neighbours' nerves and he is too small to mount the hens successfully. He is no use.

Olga has never learned to treat her poultry as an economic unit. She won't kill off the old ones or lock up the young ones. They roam, and lay eggs that are rarely found. They scratch up bedding plants, and sometimes get run over. Olga calls them free-range hens. She is sure they will lay better once the moult is over, but the moult, as far as Rowan is aware, has lasted for years.

Rowan hums her tune in minor key. Yet she is too drowsy, her body too warm in the sun, to bear for long the brunt of melancholy. She pulls up her skirt and closes her eyes.

The rooster has scrambled through the hedge.

He likes to scratch in the lettuce bed next door. Marian snatches the pink plastic cape. Like a bull-fighter she challenges the bird, which retreats, crowing in disorder.

"Wretched nuisance," says Marian. "The Council should put a stop to it. There's plenty of countryside for that sort of thing."

"I like a touch of country," says Dennis, scratching the back of his neck where the clipped hair itches.

"That bird started up at half-past five this morning. I was in the middle of the strangest dream. I wanted to finish it, and now I can't remember a thing about it. Doesn't it annoy you when that happens?"

"I don't dream."

"Of course you do. Everybody does. They've done experiments and proved it. The eyelids flicker."

"I never dream. I'm the one who's asleep. I should know."

"I still think you should ring the Council about those hens."

"You phone them if you're worried."

"I don't see why you always put everything on me." Marian snatches up the scissors and goes inside.

Dennis stays on the porch and watches the rooster scratch up Marian's lettuces.

I thought I heard someone singing in the garden," Paul suggests.

"Rowan; my eldest. It's her day off. She's a nurse."

"How many children do you have?"

There are bumps outside. A child in a nightdress backs over the doorstep, dragging a doll's pram in which sits a glaring ginger cat in a blue bonnet.

"Rowan, and Stefan; and this is Lilah," informs Olga with pride. The child assesses Paul. "Our bathroom had a flood. The hot pipe broke."

"One of our minor catastrophes," laughs Olga.

Taking its chance, the cat springs. The bonnet ribbons lash the floor. Lilah moves, swift and determined. The cat is replaced and tucked in firmly with a bath towel. Olga demurs.

"I *am* gentle, Olga. Are you the new boarder? I hope you are. Olga will cook nicer meals and Steffie will stop wetting the bed. Olga says it's the atmosphere in the home and we need a man about the place."

Paul isn't used to feeling needed. The note Linda left when she went off with the voluntary counsellor from the Community House said she would always respect his sincerity, his generosity and his good nature. These compliments have continued to worry Paul, who sensed Linda's disappointment in him long before she went. If you could only be more . . . she once suggested, but gave no further clarification. Paul hadn't known how to be other than he was; which was, by deduction, less. She'd been pleasantly bossy. He felt helpless when she left.

"We had a boarder who hit Olga and we had to ring up the police," says Lilah charmingly. She has a presence; her speeches linger.

"Take Tiger for a walk." Olga's tone is clear. Lilah bestows a *prima donna* smile and makes her exit, lugging the pram, which lacks back wheels.

Paul is feeling at home. The house has invited him in. Rambling and run-down, it titillates his imagination. Some houses are too functional and have no rooms for dreams. Paul has a dream. He wants to write and, with the compulsory sick leave attendant on his damaged liver, intends to. He tells Olga. She is thrilled.

"How well we shall get along. I read and sew and paint and am never for an instant bored, although I never have a sou."

Trying to pin her down to the conditions of his board and lodging, Paul has to conclude she is more interested in his writing aspirations, his dreams of towers. It puzzles him, this capricious attitude. Here she is in her ankle socks, pouring from an antique silver teapot, not bothered with talk of work or money, sharing in his hopes. Paul relaxes. He stretches his long legs, leans his head back against clasped hands and forgets about the time.

At last, at last, it's time to discuss business.

"You shall have the tower," Olga says, and Paul feels excited, as though his dream will materialise and explain itself. His towers are secretive and often have no entrance. He follows Olga along a narrow corridor. They pass untidy bedrooms and a bathroom draped with towels reading *N.Z. Towel Supply.* At the end of the passage a ladder leads to a square gap in the dirty ceiling. Olga nimbly mounts the rungs.

The ladder pleases Paul, who can see himself, Jack intent on giants, a suitcase anchored over the hole in the clouds, keeping fast his privacy. Olga shouts, "Catch!" A rain of sandshoes, cushions, empty food tins, shawls and paperbacks descends. "Rowan's," calls down Olga.

"Won't she mind?" asks doubtful Paul.

"She won't like you," agrees Lilah. She has come to add her weight to the inspection. "She hates boarders who leave smelly socks on the floor."

Olga disagrees. "She won't mind a bit. She's hardly ever here. She can bunk in Lilah's den for the odd night." Like Rapunzel, she peers down, playful, her faded plait dangling as though she believes her part in fairy tale. Paul smiles back and negotiates the ladder.

It is a roundish room, uncurtained. It is warm and light. The sky presses on the windowpanes. Paul gazes over the wild garden, its interlocking fruit trees, hints of lawn and former flower beds. Olga comes to stand beside him. "How overgrown it is!" Once in a while she notices. "Are you a gardener?"

Paul says no. Already he is feeling possessive and wants things kept just as they are.

"There's heaps of furniture in the shed, you know. Perhaps with a pulley . . ."

"I like it as it is." He detests clutter. "Really, it's ideal." A mattress, a rug, a strand of wire from which to hook his clothes—for the first time in weeks he is happy, discovering how Linda's departure has set him free from posters, plaques, ash-trays, photos, vases, jugs; and the pot-plants, spilling from shelves, nestling in corners, insinuating themselves behind the refrigerator, sprouting on the cistern. Plants belong outside, thinks Paul; and there is no one to disagree with him.

"Who's that?" he asks, looking towards the peach trees, letting his hand rest on the sill. Its surface feels warm. Its crazy-paved surface gives out a mellow aroma.

Olga peers down at the orchard. "Rowan. My daughter, Rowan," Olga says.

Rowan, eighteen, is training to be a psychiatric nurse. Part of the course centres on counselling and group techniques, and there is the inevitable backwash of such examination. Dipping into the psyche may fascinate Rowan but Olga has her doubts. She has never felt inclined towards self-analysis; a preoccupation, in her opinion, of idle and neurotic people. Her canvas is history, pageantry and art. The personal bores her, and she can't be bothered with boredom, be it sewing on buttons, paying bills, or dragging up the past.

She adores her children. What is this newfangled probing her eldest daughter puts her through, every time she comes home from the hospital? Rowan is her angel, the support of her life. Why this obsession with the past, with departed fathers, cast-off religions? It was better when Rowan ran about in Roman sandals and came to Olga for cuddles and Vicks VapoRub.

Hardly one hour ago there was yet another encounter.

"Wasn't I at a convent when I started school?"

"Indeed you were."

"Why was I moved?"

"Because I decided to move you."

"It must have been about the same time Dad left home?"

Olga had to sigh, for what answer was there to such probing? After the initial insult of his disappearance, she discovered it wasn't such a tragedy to lose a husband. She'd not loved him, really, for it turned out she was happier without him. She no longer had to resent his crude manners or his women. She'd yearned for children; well, she had them. He never came round to interfere, or upset them. It was only when officialdom or her children brought up the subject that she even remembered she'd been married.

"What actually happened? Why did Dad go off like that and never even write a line?"

"We simply drifted." Olga found her reply quite satisfying but Rowan frowned. "By the way . . ." Olga sensed a way to get Rowan out of the dead past and into more pressing affairs, "I wonder, darling, could I borrow? The plumber's getting very nasty."

At which point Rowan removed herself to the orchard.

Stefan comes home in the minibus run by the Special School.

The driver knows the road well. He swings round the last bend, skidding a bit on the loose gravel, and stops outside the beheaded letter-box of Number Twenty-five. He jumps out and unlocks the exit door. Steffie puts two feet on the top step, hops to the second step on his left foot, hops to the ground on his right foot, puts both feet down and stares up at the pink house, where Olga stands waving from the porch. Steffie waves and is running, his arms and legs all angles, up the track towards her. The bus skids and raises dust. Already it is out of sight, a fading grumble around the corner.

It is half past three.

In her sleep, Rowan stirs. Nursing is hard work and unrequited love is tiring. Rowan sleeps on, dreaming of a lake, a yacht with a red sail, black swans on an emerald hill.
It was windy beside the lake. Her hair blew in her face and she laughed.
"When you were a tiny you ran right into the breakers, never mind they bowled you every time," her father said. She knew that today he liked her a lot. He did like people who were bold. Isobel, who he'd held hands with in the pictures, was like that. Well, it was fun, the pictures and ferry ride and bus, and now the picnic.
Isobel smiled and said, "Here love, have a Golden Queen." Rowan bit the peach and in her mouth there was a shock, and fur, and sticky on her chin. Isobel spat on the corner

of her hanky but Rowan turned away her head. "I can do it."

Dad laughed. "'Little tyke. How old are you?"

"I'm seven." He forgot things people should remember. He'd say, Who cares? when Olga ticked him off, and laughed when she said he had no education and no manners.

"Seven?" He grabbed her and he spun her and her skirt filled and rippled like the boat's sail.

"Put me down!" she screamed, loving his bigness. He teased, saying he would throw her to the swans. His cruel black moustache came close to scrape her neck. She smelled him, smoky, as he nuzzled her and set her on her feet.

Birds, big black birds, were leaving the lake and starting to come up the hill. Their feathers were shining, their necks were reaching and searching. Rowan held tight to Dad's hand. He laughed at her. "They're after some tucker."

"We ate it all," she said. It was good when he took her with him, but sometimes things happened and she wished she'd stayed with Olga and baby Steffie instead. Dad liked brave people. He chose Rowan to take on the dodgem cars, into the surf, down caves where it was dark and wetas lived on the walls.

"Better eat my fingers then." He let the swans peck his hand. Rowan felt shivery. "I'll get the scraps." She ran to ask Isobel, but they could only find a packet of marshmallows. Rowan wanted them for herself. She went back slowly.

It was just starting to rain. The biggest bird put up his wings. They made a dark hood, like Olga's black umbrella. He was making runs at the others. Feathers came out. The weak ones ran away. It was like the film, when the soldiers shouted, "Charge!" Open red beaks were near. Their noise was out-of-breath and strange, and made her

afraid. The pink and white marshmallows fell on the ground and she called out, "Dad!"
He was there and she was high, above the grass, above the swans. She could see the top of his head where the curly black hair was thinner, and she wasn't frightened of anything. Dad set her down and tore a marshmallow to bits and showed her how to hold them on her flat palm, and they fed the swans together.
It started raining hard. Isobel came running, and told them to come under the pine tree. Dad wouldn't, so Isobel just laughed, and gave him a kiss, the rain running down her face, and she took Rowan to shelter. They pressed against the pine trunk side by side. Isobel said, "Lovey, has your Dad told you about him and me?" Rowan said no. "We're going to go away and live together," Isobel said. Rowan rubbed the goose-bumps on her arms and asked if she was going too. "You can't," Isobel said, hugging her, "because there's your Mum and the baby, and your Dad says it's best you stay with them." They watched the lake. "I'll be coming to stay," Rowan said. "Course you will," said Isobel.
Dad came running under the tree, and Isobel tried to dry him with her poncho. She said, "I told her," and Dad said, "Told her what?" and Isobel said, "You should have," and Dad said, "How was it?" and Isobel said, "All right. I think she knew." Dad hugged Rowan. She smelled him in the warm, wet clothes, and held on tight, and wouldn't let go. He ruffled up her hair, the way he touched her if she fell down and hurt herself.
They dashed through the rain to the bus stop. The three of them squashed up in a seat for two. The bus window went foggy and Rowan drew houses with her finger. They got off at Isobel's and she gave them crumpets and cups of tea. Dad and Isobel wanted to have a rest, and Rowan fell asleep, too, on the couch by the heater.

Rowan comes inside.

She has two mosquito bites on her cheek and she is not pleased to meet Paul, who has been allocated her tower room while she slept. She sniffs. "I suppose it's curry?"

"I burned it, darling," Olga says placatingly.

According to the marble mantel clock it's time for Paul to catch his bus. Olga won't let him out of her sight unless first he stays and eats, to put a seal upon the contract.

"What can we have to celebrate?" She searches her cane basket for her purse. "I think we all deserve a treat. Show Paul where to find the dairy, Rowan, and choose whatever you like."

"I'll buy baked beans." Rowan will not be won over. Silently she walks out into the lemony washings of afternoon light, Paul following. Quite soon he's out of breath and has to call a halt. "He's not very fit," thinks Rowan, feeling disarmed.

Strong, bad-tempered Angelo, who boarded with the family for four tempestuous years, overpowered proud Olga in a way Rowan came to fear. Paul won't be like that. He is too reserved, too quiet, to wield dark, disruptive power. It's hard to resent him when now she sees he's not well. He looks in need of care, of mothering. It's not his fault that Olga put him in the tower.

"I'm sorry I've got your room," he says. "I've been sick, you see, and I need a place that's quiet. But I'm sure I could manage somewhere else."

"I'm not home all that often," Rowan says.

Paul walks slowly, taking in sap-scents and the glint and shade of leaf. "You know, I can't believe I'm going to live here."

Rowan's lived there longer, and in the winter. "Mmm . . . it's a rotten bus service, and miles to carry things."

"You really mind about the buses?"

"Olga does. She'd like to move."

"Then I hope it's not for ages. It feels like home to me."

"Where's home?" asks Rowan.

And Paul, who had the answer off pat when he was five (Paul-Turner-One-Three-Six-Fraser-Street-Tauranga) hardly knows how to reply. Life was clearer when he was a child. In Fraser Street nothing was uncertain.

Fraser Street was long and straight, and its houses fair and square. When it rained in Fraser Street, the rain ran neatly in the gutters, and neatly down the drains. Cars knew where to park. Flowers made petals and dropped them at the right time. The estuary water knew when to cover up the mud, and when to let it show. Everything in Fraser Street had its time and place.

Big trees grew along the verge beside the paddocks. First there were green leaves. Then they went yellow and came off. The branches stuck out, bare. Round green balls grew instead. They fell down and hit Paul on the head. They smelled of lemons. They tasted nasty, and stained his hands. He opened them every season. Always he found the big black nut, never any good to eat. There were the other trees. One had big leaves which went dry and rattled, and the wind scattered them. Then red berries came in bunches shaped like the grapes on the garage wall at home. One kept its leaves and they were curved and spiky, like a dragon's comb. Some were thin, pale-barked trees with gentle leaves. The trees never really changed. Paul trusted them. When he went to Intermediate School there were nature walks. Then he learned the names of the trees, and things about them. South African Black Nut, that was good for timber. Idesias, they needed a mate. Phoenix Palms were evergreen, and Silver Birch, deciduous. The teacher always taught about the outsides of the trees. Paul understood they had an inside life that mattered more.

"I was born in Tauranga," Paul says. "Not a bit like Titirangi. Though there were trees."

The bush discloses wing-beats, lumbering, then rushing as the wood-pigeon leaves cover, climbs above the kauris, plummets. Paul stands still. He turns to Rowan, wanting to make friends with her. She smiles. She has forgiven him.

They walk on to the shop, their footsteps falling in companionable rhythm. A fantail flicks and dives beside them. Paul has read they follow people for the insects their passage disturbs, but he imagines the bush has sent its spirit, an escort assuring him he's welcome.

TWO

Living on the fringe of heaven, Olga's translation of *Titirangi,* has been a mixed blessing.

Washing sags from the line for weeks in winter. Her asthma gets worse when it rains, and in Titirangi it often rains. The heating bills are huge, the bus service is erratic, and any part-time work goes to those with private transport. In any case, Olga doesn't want to work. She thinks money is a commodity and she treats it with the caprice and disdain commodities deserve. To serve in a shop or do housework and be paid for it is, in her view, boring, although she would do it for nothing if someone were ill. Of this particular commodity Olga is undoubtedly short. Yet she wants help from no one. To neighbours who bring cartons of used clothing or bags of seasonal grapefruit she is gracious. She serves tea in the Royal Doulton cups and discusses the post-impressionists until her well-wishers shift uncomfortably and go home. Olga is suspicious of people who give her things. She thinks they want a foothold in her life. Let them find some other family to help. Olga, who has seen Margot Fonteyn dance, needs no charity. She has tried to pass on her values to her children. They know about *suburbia*—coloured roof tiles, and a plush lounge suite from the *Farmers*. When it is time to run for buckets and bowls to place under the leaks in the old iron roof, they seem to agree it's not important, in spite of Olga's grumbles.

Between Olga and her children there is an atmosphere of a delicious secret, a conspiracy. Do other mothers colour the mashed potato green, when there is nothing else for dinner, or light candles and play at Pioneers when the power board is mean about the bills? Sometimes the Cross prevails, and Olga feels bitter; but as a rule fate is her plaything.

She has had eleven years to find herself. When her husband left, she was for a short time a Deserted Wife. She soon gave up that role. Her asthma improved without his insinuations of other women, confident women, who presumably accorded him pleasures Olga could not, so that her ribs squeezed hard and her nostrils drew pinched breaths. She could retaliate well enough with her tongue, but Olga preferred civilized conversation to a slanging match. When he set her free, she discovered her own resentment fading, and she was grateful.

It took time to deal with material problems, though. He sent no money. Expert though she was, robbing Peter, juggling Paul, treating herself to a little luxury now and then, she couldn't make ends meet. There were interminable delays with the Welfare Department. She realised she had to have more money somehow. She had never been to work. Since disagreeing with the perspectives of the university syllabus and tossing in a half-completed Arts degree, she had survived without a job. She had studied and painted and kept her home clean and her children cared for and the herbs growing. The idea of routine appalled her. She didn't mind being on the bread line.

Yet she had to get a job—to tide us over, as she comforted herself; even feeling excited at the prospect of a new experience. She imagined some discreet, congenial position. She rang the Museum. They were pleasant and polite, but her qualifications weren't good enough. She rang the owner of a music shop. Her enunciation and her knowledge of classical music impressed him and he offered her an interview; but Olga in beaded cardigan and caftan, without the slightest interest in stocktaking or invoicing, didn't get the job. The manager of the Cosmo Print and Litho Centre felt the same. Olga went back to the Situations Vacant columns.

She went for an interview as a cook in an Old Folks' Home in Herne Bay. The place was dark and stank of urine. Bed-ridden old women were packed four to a lino-floored room. The mobile ones were propped in vinyl-covered arm-chairs in the sitting room. The job entailed split shifts—a few hours off after lunch, back mid-afternoon to get the night meal underway. The old ladies had to be fed early so the staff could get them into bed before they went off duty at six p.m. Olga watched cockroaches hurtle over the benches and declined the job. Going home, the bus was full and she had to stand. Her purse was empty. They had sandwiches minus the filling for tea.

Olga applied for a job in a sheet and towel factory. The personnel manager was at a loss. Olga dressed oddly and looked poor, yet she held a partial Arts degree. Regarding the job, she seemed flippant. He asked whether she really wanted to work with the firm, and Olga could not truthfully say that she did. It was money she wanted, though she seemed not quite convinced, even about that. Her inner belief was the Lord provides, even if at the present moment there was some hitch with the delivery. No, Olga really didn't want to hem sheets. She preferred to study Etruscan architecture and Renaissance art, to paint streaky landscapes in oils. She liked to be with her children; not infrequently kept them away from school for minor ailments because she wanted their company. Olga's sympathies lay entirely with the poor and needy, but she didn't want to queue with them, day in, day out, for a seat on the workers' bus.

She missed that job. The cats had picked four nights running at plain boiled rice, and were frantic with hunger. Rowan had no shoes, and herbs weren't helping Steffie's cough. Olga set her shoulders under the plastic raincoat and went for a job cleaning Council restrooms. When she was quizzed she presented fewer reservations than usual, saying nothing about dependent children or distance from the city. She looked bedraggled, her pride reduced by facts and the unseasonable rain. She agreed humbly and cheerfully that she felt capable of minding the restrooms, cleaning floors and toilets, giving change and keeping an eye on things. The storm had reduced the applicants to an Asian immigrant who spoke no English, a sad woman whose breath at ten in the morning smelled of sherry, and Olga. Olga was employed.

At first she didn't mind. Miscast as char-lady, she played the part as someone else might take a job as Santa Claus. She put on a pink overall and pushed the wheeled bucket from cubicle to cubicle, stripping her mop through the rollers and plying its steaming strings like some Gargantuan paintbrush.

For Steffie she had to find a baby-sitter. She thought of Mrs. Patel, a recently made friend. Olga had met Asha and her husband in the dairy, asked them home for a cup of tea, and subsequently helped them through the anxieties of foreign social customs and their first experience of winter. Asha sat nervous and silent, pleating her sari folds; but Chunilal had more fluent English and more enterprise. With Olga's permission, he gathered manuka from the back of her section and chopped it up, and shared the load with her. Their daughter Hanu sometimes came to play with Rowan after school. Asha became less shy, arriving with *chapattis* to sit in Olga's living room and admire with sighs and gestures the family heirlooms Olga treasured. Olga showed her the photo albums and Asha turned their pages with respect. It was Olga's first winter without her husband, and she had long since written off the neighbours. She was glad of company as humble and undemanding as Asha's.

Asha agreed to mind Steffie while Olga was at work, and Rowan went to the restrooms after school if Olga had to work a late shift. She liked going. She felt at home beside the heater, watching the milk-skin wrinkle as the cocoa cooled. She was familiar with this atmosphere; without men, close to the ordinary aspects of life. The pull-chains made a homely clank behind closed doors. She could hear the traffic's roar overhead; underground was like a cave, and safe. Women took off their formal manners below street level. They hitched at their skirts and tugged at their seams, communing with mirror-selves as they worked combs and lipstick. They would put on their city expressions and tap on high heels up the steps.

Rowan stayed behind the glass partition and looked at her books while Olga did her work. Olga would come to sit with her then, and the office would smell of Jeypine disinfectant and clothing wintered in a damp wardrobe. People wanting coins to open the lavatory door would tap on the glass, and Olga would smile, cross-legged on the cushion playing Snakes and Ladders or showing Rowan how to do French knitting on a cotton reel, and scramble to her feet. Her ball of wool would roll away across the lino as she counted out change, her demeanour that of a good neighbour pleased to lend a cup of sugar.

Olga liked many people individually and loved everyone *en masse.* It was only the well-to-do who gave her trouble. She was poor. She knew it and she didn't mind it. Her desire for rare and precious objects she attributed to a respect for antiquity and values which endured. Because she truly felt the material was immaterial, she couldn't conceive herself to be materialistic. The rich were satisfyingly impersonal. Olga couldn't abide wealth. It so rarely went with taste. The price of its acquisition was often a narrow-minded obsession, and ugly reminders of its presence. For Olga, no electrical wonders, no wall-to-wall carpets, no petrol-consuming monster with noxious breath to pollute the precious air; for Olga, breakdowns and bus queues and heavy shopping bags to weight her with resentment. Most passers-by, noting her defiant posture and the toss of her head, did not dare to stop and offer her a lift. Olga said she didn't care, that charity was the hobby of nosy-parkers and those who nursed a guilty conscience. She didn't want it, her desires were in another realm.

Pursuing them, she had become a convert to the Catholic church. Its complexity enthralled her; its rules did not. When she turned her back on it, her heart bled—pageantry, art, music, history, all lost along with her faith. Nursing a small and unacknowledged bitterness, Olga moved on through brotherhoods and splinter sects, through Western and Eastern philosophies. Putting the same investment in each one, she decided they were all the same. Like the stack of bills in her dresser drawer, their claims and details might vary but the expectation was the same. They were all after her money, her time, and a fair part of her freedom. They were cluttered up with people, and people usually well-fed, well-heeled, and well-informed upon Society and the rights and wrongs thereof. Olga chose to thumb her nose at the lot of them, though she never refused any keyhole peep into the insubstantial world. She had visited palmists and Tarot readers. A colour therapist had visualised her aura, and Steffie had been prayed over by a faith healer. Olga had tried to contact grandmother Julia through a medium with whom she had a short, intense friendship. Grandmother had hovered but not come through and the medium had moved on, leaving Olga with a familiar sense of frustration. So often she had felt herself to be on the brink of a revelation whose meaning she would understand only after she had experienced it. She could neither doubt its existence nor confirm its reality.

Working at the restrooms had several advantages. For a weekly income of assured if only moderate amount, she was dependent on no vagaries of male mood, nor on any suggestion that she owed a certain gratitude for that support. She was earning the money herself and she could do what she liked with it. But problems arose. The Patels were offered accommodation in the inner city with relatives from the Gujarat. Asha and Chunilal came to exchange addresses and press Olga's hand, sorrier to say goodbye to her than to the dripping Titirangi bush. At the same time Rowan went down with bronchitis. Olga had to take a few days off work to nurse her, and find someone else to babysit for Steffie. A less willing friend agreed; the arrangement, it was made clear, being strictly temporary.

The return to her old routine reminded Olga how much she preferred to be at home with her children, painting, pottering about the house and garden. She pampered Rowan with sugared lemon drinks and eucalyptus inhalations; Rowan not minding the fuss. As Olga's most independent child she was often treated more as a proxy younger sister and confidante of her mother. Her cough soon disappeared. Olga took her back to work reluctantly. She washed floors while Rowan filled the soap dispensers and hung up new toilet rolls. Olga plugged in the heater in the office and prepared to make cocoa on the tiny camp stove. Feeling in need of a treat to dull her worry at leaving Steffie in less than ideal circumstances, she reached into her ancient handbag and gave several coins to Rowan. "Whip over to the NibbleNook and get some Fruit and Nut," suggested Olga, and Rowan grabbed her coat and went.

Near the stair exit, she saw a man lying on the footpath. Rain fell lightly down on him. He did not seem to notice. Rowan crossed the road and bought the chocolate and crossed back again. He was still there. She skipped down the restroom steps.

"There's a man lying up there." Rowan pointed, and Olga set down the cocoa packet.

"We'd better investigate," she said.

As she gazed at the figure which lay unconscious on the footpath, drizzle powdering his black hair and beard, Olga was moved by compassion and attraction. During her Catholic period she had often made the Stations of the Cross, genuflecting before each of the fourteen depictions of Jesus' passion and death. Now she did not recognise the feeling of self-abnegation those paintings of the abandoned Christ had stirred in her. This man lay in the rain, unaware of her yet dependent on her, his attitude reflecting indifference to any woman's caring. Olga decided it was only common kindness to move a helpless fellow being out of the rain.

"Is he drunk?" Rowan asked.

"The police will have him in the lock-up quick smart if he is," said Olga, coming to a decision. "He might be ill. You take his feet."

"Are we allowed to take him down?" Rowan pointed out the sign saying *Women*.

"He's not going to care," Olga said, "and neither do I. I've got most of the weight. You pull a bit—he should slide down."

Rowan had to feel impressed at the strength of her slender mother, and the efficiency with which she had her bundle arranged on the office floor, her rolled-up cardigan tucked beneath his head. "What are we going to do now?" she asked.

"He'll wake up sooner or later." Olga felt a kind of elation, and she signalled to the chocolate bar. "Open the Fruit and Nut," she said.

When Angelo woke up and discovered he was in a Ladies' Restroom, ministered to by pink-overalled Olga, he felt obliged to explain himself. "To lie like a deadbeat in the gutter—how must it look? If I have any excuse, it is this. For ten years I look after my mother and now she is dead. Her stomach swells up, she can't walk. We go to the hospital. They put her to bed and they sew in her belly a tube to drain away the water. The doctors say it is a blockage. I visit her. She looks up at me with her tired, sad eyes, and she says, 'Dio mio, Angelo, you can put me under the ground now.' I say to her, 'No, Mamma, you are a fighter. Remember in Italy, all those years ago, paying off the family debts, how you sold firewood, carried great loads up the stairs on your own back? How you helped Papa build our house? I saw you cart the buckets of cement myself. You can still fight.' She just says, 'I'm tired. Your papa died in this hospital of the lung sickness, and I'm going to die here too.'

"The nurse comes in. She says, 'Get out of bed please, Mrs. Guzzo, you need to take some exercise.'

Mamma says No, she doesn't want exercise. 'I'm old. Is come, my time for dying.' I like this nurse. She doesn't put you off, pretend she doesn't hear. She sits on Mamma's bed and takes her wrinkled hand. 'Are you afraid?' she asks. Mamma gives her one of her looks. 'I no afraid,' says Mamma. The nurse persuades her to get up. We walk a little bit. I hold Mamma's one arm and the nurse holds the other. I think Mamma seems not so sick. Her stomach is big like she is having a baby, but she doesn't seem so bad. I ask the nurse later. Out by the lifts we talk. 'Maybe my mother is sick from bad food? All the biscuits and the Coca Cola? She never eats a proper meal any more.' The nurse shakes her head. Not the biscuits. 'You know, Mamma is like a child a little bit. She opened every Coca Cola in the crate, didn't finish one, just drank a sip from each.' 'It's not her diet,' says the nurse. 'I think she's very sick.' I nod. 'I think so,' I say. I feel now that Mamma is going to die. The nurse can read my thoughts, and she touches my arm. 'You care for your mother very much,' she says, 'it's unusual.' 'In Italy we care for the old parents.' 'How come you haven't got married yourself?' 'With Mamma, it's no good bringing in a girl. I tried it.' The nurse laughs with me. 'What do you do then, in your spare time?' 'What spare time? My spare times goes to her. I feed her, wash her. She grumbles. Why do the old not like to wash? I warm the towel for her, the way she used to do for me. In the morning she says, "I slept like a bambino, Angelo. But no bath today, eh?"'

"So I leave and drive my van home, and the house is empty and quiet, Mamma gone and no love there. They ring me in the night to tell me. She died in her sleep, like a bambino. That was one week ago, and every day I think, What am I going to do with Mamma dead?"

Olga decided there was every reason for him to be drunk. She made him a cup of tea and helped him to drink it, steadying the cup. When he murmured, to himself or to Olga, "Where am I to go?" she beamed and said assertively, "Why, home with us." Even Rowan knew you couldn't pick up a man like a stray pup you might adopt because it seemed to have lost its way. She waited for Angelo to refuse. He hardly seemed to see Olga as he pressed her hand against his pale, exhausted-looking face. "I never wish to see Mamma's house again. Please wake me when it is time to leave." His head on the cardigan, he closed his eyes and seemed to sleep immediately.

Angelo's entry into Olga's household coincided with her departure from the restrooms. Someone wanting change had looked through the office window, seen a man asleep on the floor and made a complaint to the Council. Olga was brought to task and asked to make an explanation. She did, honestly and without embellishment. She was not believed. She was given notice.

Olga didn't mind. With Angelo made comfortable in the tower room and board agreed upon, she felt sure she could manage financially. Angelo worked for a firm which supplied linen and laundry service to commercial firms. A van went with the job, so there was no longer a need to carry groceries. Angelo seemed very happy to be needed. Olga was a few years older than he was, yet curiously childlike, as his mother had become in later life. Her children seemed to him to be in need of discipline; he thought Olga spoilt them. There was no set bedtime or appointed chores such as he remembered from his earliest years. Rowan addressed her mother as "Olga," which suggested disrespect to Angelo. He decided there was a great deal needed from him in the household.

Olga was delighted with Angelo. He was serious, in contrast to her playful attitude to life. At first she adopted a maternal role with him, making his dinner, mending his clothes. She sent him off to work with the same well-wishing wave she gave Rowan when she left for school. Olga's concern helped Angelo through his bereavement, but her own needs saw to it that their relationship quickly became more complex. Angelo was strong and responsible. He could carry things, shift things, repair things. He made Rowan dry the dishes.

Angelo came from a world of clear-cut values dictated by matters of money, tradition and commitment to family. Men should support their wives, wives should have their babies, children should respect their parents, and everybody should keep the law. While his attitudes seemed repressive to Olga, they were curiously safe, and for a time they suited her. For the first time in her life she knew exactly where she stood. Angelo's needs were simple and, as long as she met them, Angelo was willing to do innumerable small jobs for her. He was handy with tools, electrical wiring, paintbrushes. The house began to look cared for. Angelo climbed on the roof and delved down to the poor foundations. He worked quickly and with endurance. Olga felt inspired to make new curtains for the windows whose cracked panes Angelo replaced. She cleaned the oven while he renewed the elements. Angelo attacked the garden with pitchfork and scythe. Precious cuttings, whose whereabouts underneath the weeds were known only to Olga, disappeared. She didn't dare complain. Within weeks the lawn resembled a paddock after hay-making. Angelo proudly flexed his arm. Demure Olga provided pasta for the evening meal. Standing beside him to serve his food, she commented on his strength. He ate the pasta in silence but she knew he liked her praise. He ruled the table less paternalistically and didn't reprove Rowan when she declined the macaroni.

Rowan was less impressed with Angelo. He made rules without consulting her—something Olga never did. He wasn't interested in her point of view, implying she was too young and unimportant to have anything worthwhile to say. There was neither flexibility nor fun in the chores he allocated. He did not praise her for a job well done but brought her back to repeat work he considered shoddy. He made her do homework every night and lectured her on the benefits of education. Steffie was young enough to escape Angelo's censure. He cried for Olga when Angelo patted his head, awkwardly, not knowing how a man might come down to the level of a bambino.

"Why do we have to have Angelo here?" Rowan complained to Olga after he had shouted at her to get off her lazy backside and feed the hens when Olga told her to.

"Angelo is paying for your new shoes on Friday night," said comforting Olga.

"I don't want them." Although she did. She longed for new clothes, beautiful dresses, patent-leather shoes. On Friday they went in the van to the shopping centre and walked to the shoe shop, Angelo striding ahead like Moses, his followers behind. New shoes were bought; of good quality leather, with thick soles and sturdy laces, bound to last.

"I hate Angelo," complained Rowan, after he had forced her to sit on at table after the others had finished. "I hate that slimy pasta you always cook now. I hate garlic and tomato skins."

"They're good for you, darling."

Rowan scowled. Olga despised health foods and diet fads and had never been known to put forward, as a reason for doing anything, that it was "good for you." The reply was Angelo's.

Angelo wasn't entirely unknowledgeable in those matters of culture so dear to Olga's heart. He had a cassette recorder installed in the van. As he went from office-block to shop, delivering fresh bags of linen, taking away the dirty towels, he played Beethoven, Mahler. His taste ran to the sombre, with undertones of passion.

Angelo, who in his mother's dependent years had attended all her most private and personal bodily needs, never allowed himself to dwell on images he would describe as sinful. Permitted to look without shame on her body, Angelo never let his thoughts fantasise on young or willing women similarly exposed. He had been trained to keep impure thoughts at bay and that is what he did. He drove the same way, his foot ready for the brake.

He was aware of his effect on Olga's household; less so of the insidious changes taking place within himself. In this tumbledown house on a hill there were laughter and children's footsteps and Olga, forgetting her dignity and doing the cake-walk in a kimono bought for a song at the Opportunity Shop. There were play fights and real fights and disconcerting attitudes, to bills, bedtimes, ideas of right and wrong which until then Angelo had considered inviolate. Olga just laughed at him when he said it was shocking that people did such things, that such things were printed in the newspaper.

"What things?" Olga wanted to make him say, although he knew she'd seen the article on suburban wife-swapping. He blushed to think of it, and Olga laughed again and said, "People pay sex far too much attention. Animals have the right attitude."

Olga's cats were constantly in kitten. Angelo continued to blush. Such things were never spoken about by Mamma, although such things were understood between them. Olga had no time for such things. She called a spade a spade, and sex, sex. Angelo began to think of Olga in a way that would have shocked Mamma, for it shocked him. He thought of her at night. Instead of sleeping, as normal people do after an honest day's work and an evening's relaxation, Angelo imagined himself taking off Olga's clothes, and his, and doing such things to her, and with her, as his repressed imagination of twenty-nine years finally displayed to him. He listened for her footsteps, in case she padded to the bathroom; often she could not last a whole night long without relieving her bladder, which she'd airily told him had been a Woolworth's job ever since she had the children. In Angelo's mind he followed her there, and watched as she sat on the lavatory seat, and listened as the water she made splashed and trickled in the pan.

Angelo tried praying, a habit he'd given up after Mamma grew too old to go to Mass and he no longer went along to please, and keep her company. Bad-tempered, he got up in the mornings, avoiding Olga in her torn candlewick dressing gown which revealed the fragile hollows of her neck. He shouted at Rowan and kicked the cats out of the way when they rubbed against him, wanting breakfast scraps. He went for walks. Eventually he shamed himself as he'd not done since Mamma's death. He got drunk, not helplessly drunk, but drunk enough to fall over, coming in the door. Olga helped him to his feet. She looked uncertain, reminded as she was of her husband's drunken bouts, abuse and pain.

Angelo was not abusive. On the contrary, his appreciation of Olga's helping hand astonished her. He murmured words she could only assume to be endearments; although she could not translate his slurred Italian, his expression spoke for him. She helped him along the passage, cast her eye over the vertical ladder leading up to his room, and decided he was in no state to manage the climb. She took him into her boudoir—it was exactly that; an intimate woman's room, furnished with the very best of grandmother's inheritance, the tapestry chaise longue, the standard lamps, the inlaid walnut writing desk. Olga drew the curtains to cover the ugly louvred windows, and turned the lamp-light on.

Angelo stood uncertainly on the fading Turkish rug. He stumbled across to Olga's bed and lay down, letting dizzy waves of guilt and desire accost him. Olga looked down at him. She saw the man who lay in the rain in need. Sympathy and self-abnegation welled up at the picture of him, a grown man twice her size, several times her strength, vulnerable to her. His beery smell and tousled hair only increased her desire to soothe him, give to him, and take away his loneliness and need.

Carefully she sat on the edge of the bed and began to stroke his forehead. Angelo accepted her. She leaned down and softly kissed his closed eyes. A profound tenderness engulfed her as he lay submissive. She stretched out beside him and drew his head against her breast, and let him reach inside and touch her skin and feel her body. They lay like that for a while. At last Angelo fell asleep.

A soft, expectant atmosphere came over the household after that night. Angelo bought aluminum saucepans for Olga and new shirts for himself. He became patient with the children. Olga wore perfume, and said she longed to brush up her amateur Italian. She fetched *A New Italian Reader For Beginners* and sat at his feet after dinner. She read aloud, extracts from *Peppino Il Lustrascarpe*, or *La Medicina*, Angelo correcting her pronunciation. They read *L'Osteria Della Posta* together, Angelo looking over her shoulder and taking the male parts. Olga played the Countess. They laughed a lot.

Olga invited Angelo to listen to the ancient gramophone she kept in her room. Angelo sat on the chaise longue, his eyes filling with tears as Olga played her 78s of *Aida* and *La Traviata*. It would grow late and one of them would play another record, not wanting to break that close, suspended state.

It was Olga who finally owned up to herself that, if Angelo wanted her, she wanted him. She suggested he might like to come to her room that night after the children were in bed. He sensed a choice and felt anxious. He preferred situations to happen to him, as their first encounter had happened. Angelo believed he was a good man; by which he meant a moral man, a keeper of the law. He knew Olga was separated from her husband, but his Church had no interest in matters of proximity or non-proximity. Marriage was for ever and even after death. Angelo considered the implications of adultery and apologised to Mamma who, he felt, hovered. "I will be strong, Mamma," he promised. It was after all easier to do nothing. He lay awake all night. In the room below his, so did Olga.

As the hours passed, her state of mind shifted from eagerness to anger to self-criticism. For wasn't she older than he was, with a body used in childbearing, and breasts small and flat? She felt unfit for him. She'd watched as he worked, his shirt off, in the sun. Olga lay in the dark, feeling rejected and, for the first time in her life, old.

In the morning she silently served breakfast to a silent Angelo. Wheezing a little, she excused herself from the customary ritual of farewell and went back to bed. Angelo knew he had offended her. He thought of her waiting for him, imagining he was unable to behave as healthy men do with a woman. She might pity him. Certainly she must despise him. He went off to work quietly, feeling none of the satisfaction a moral man surely deserved. A week went by. Olga served mince and roast beef, which Rowan ate greedily. When she made a mistake, practising her Italian, she blushed instead of laughing. She went to bed early, and did not play the gramophone. Angelo couldn't understand how doing right could feel so wrong. He sensed that virtue was a more complicated issue than he had been led to believe.

Angelo made Olga a cup of tea, and knocked politely on her boudoir door. She lay against her pillows, reading Camus' *The Outsider*. She laid the book face-down and took the cup. She wore an old white nightdress, open at the throat where the buttons had come off. It was pin-tucked, lace-edged. Angelo thought she looked pure, old-fashioned. "For the Contessa." He held out the cup; an offering. She smiled, looking quietly up at him. He noticed her eyes, very dark tonight. He could not look away. He sensed he was forgiven.

Angelo had a bath. He combed his hair, and his beard, and cleaned his teeth very well. He put on his pyjamas, changed his mind and put on a clean shirt and trousers, then changed his mind again and got back into his pyjamas. He put on his dressing gown and fastened the silky cord. He went to the lavatory. He checked that the front door was locked, for Olga was very casual about locking up, saying if people needed her things they were welcome to help themselves. Angelo looked at Steffie in his cot. He checked that Rowan was asleep. He stood outside Olga's door. He felt tense, both nervous and excited. He had never made love to a woman.

Olga made it very easy. She demanded nothing. She knew what to do. Her hands spoke to him, telling him there was plenty of time. She knew touches that gave pleasure. She seemed to want to serve him. He took her love and let it fill him, and he gave it back to her and she accepted him.

Afterwards he felt happy. Olga stroked his face gently, like a child's, but he knew that in the darkness they had built a way of being together that was new. He felt loved; his body relaxed, his soul respected. She had understood his needs. He felt like a child, and like a man. Angelo patted Olga's bottom, drawing her slight frame against the stronger curving of his own. They slept a while. He went back to his own bed before morning. He thought it would be wrong, for the children to guess that such a thing had taken place.

In spite of Angelo's invasion by mortal sin, he felt at peace. Life assumed a routine that suited him. Olga was happier, the house better cared for, the children quieter. They had been lovers for six months when Olga told him she was going to have a baby. They were both delighted. Olga felt young, fed by the wellspring of fertility. Angelo felt proud. He proposed to Olga. Olga said yes. But she was a Catholic, married in a civil ceremony, and there were complications. Angelo sought legal and religious counsel and presented his findings to Olga, who listened, astonished, to his talk of divorce suits and matrimonial Church law, and said she wasn't interested in such ballyhoo.

Angelo dealt with her resistance in the way that seemed to him most natural. He ordered her to see the lawyer and the priest. Olga became the Countess. Not only did she refuse to take orders from Angelo but she also became his superior in every aspect of age, race and grace. Angelo began to feel very angry, to feel like an ordinary Italian van driver, not very clever, not with any rights, not worth much at all. He looked at Olga, her icy posture, her small, defiant body, and he thought he would like to punch her until she cried out for mercy and bowed to his indisputable strength. Angelo went away to his tower to suffer his emotions by himself. He saw how the catechism had known better than Angelo's self-love. Sin's penalty was upon him. His manhood was demeaned, his self-worth trampled on by a woman, not even a beautiful woman; all because he'd shown his weaker side and given her entry to his heart.

Surely it was a simple matter. He was not asking very much of her, inviting her to become his wife and give their baby an honourable start in life. He did not mind if she denied the Church in her heart. He, after all, was not a model Catholic. He did believe in the outward forms of religion, and consulting the priest seemed a minor matter, if then there was a chance they could be properly married. He did not demand promises or flowery declarations of love. He just wanted them to be wed, in the proper way, in the rites of his religion. He saw her refusal as stubbornness; a female control keeping him weak and untrue to his sex.

Angelo became sullen, and Olga, silent. They said no more about marriage. The baby grew, invisible yet present, like the wordless confrontation between them. Sometimes he came to her in the darkness. Then his body spoke with a changed language. He took from her with more aggression. She felt him care for her less. She submitted, as though trying to tell him their battle wasn't of themselves, not of Angelo and Olga, as much as of sex roles and resistance to some male authority—father, husband, faceless controller of her will. She tried to share her body's changes with him, wanting him to feel love for the child he had given her. He remained silent. His commitment was to his first-born received, as a child should be, with the sanctions of law and church. He wanted no bastard.

Olga became frail as the pregnancy progressed. Her body wasn't the accommodating kind, and the growing child announced its existence blatantly. Olga spent a lot of time in bed. Her cooking and housekeeping became perfunctory. Rowan perceived the division between her mother and recent oppressor and began to play one against the other. The household had lost its leadership.

Angelo stopped going to Olga's room. He missed her comfort, yet felt better in his wilful isolation. She had no hold on him this way. His deliberate sowing of withdrawal took root and flourished. He came home late, ate at cafeterias some nights. A few times he drank alone at bars, feeding harsh thoughts of loneliness and reprisal. Olga began to complain. The grass was overgrown. The painting was half finished. His board was overdue. Tangible complaints excused her feeling of rejection. He made it plain he didn't want the child unless she went, cap in hand, to investigate loopholes in church law with the priest. It might be politic to do so, but it would also be untruthful. Her integrity was at stake. She could not make him see.

Sometimes, hearing him come in late, she experienced that dread she'd felt for her husband. The door would slam, the house would fill with an aura of displeasure. She could almost have painted it, that viscous cloud of hostility. Her chest tightened, making her wheeze.

She thought he would come round after the child was born.

He was at work when Olga began labour. She pinned a message to the front door and caught a taxi to the hospital. Angelo stayed out drinking, and found the note next morning. By then the baby girl was born. By the time he visited, Olga had taken over the child as hers, entirely hers. She told him the name she had chosen—Delilah—and added firmly that there would be no christening or hocus-pocus.

Olga went home, Angelo moved out.

The baby thrived. Angelo moved in.

It had become that kind of bond; inability to come close, unwillingness to separate. Angelo discovered one way to defeat Olga and at the same time maintain that sense of unworthiness he blamed her for causing. He knew that since her choice, Olga before Angelo, he'd not felt about himself as a man should feel. They both deserved punishment. He would go out, get drunk, come home, needle her until she lashed out with her educated, hurtful tongue; then stop the flow of words, trading pain for pain. He left bruises sometimes. Proud Olga covered those she could with garments, and blamed untimely accidents for the marks she could not hide. After such an episode a sense of peace came over them both. A tension had been let go, a price paid.

Rowan would hide in the bedroom at such times, Steffie clinging to her, saying nothing, until the fracas died away.

Olga's and Angelo's way of being might have endured longer than its four-year course except for Olga's greatest strength, and weakness: her pride. Private suffering she would bear but public humiliation was another matter. He began to make their fights public, shouting and hammering on the door late at night. He bailed her up in view of the neighbour's porch and stood over her, swearing, and in English, for all the world to hear. Olga went to the phone box and telephoned the police. She displayed her bruises and cut face when they came, and Angelo was taken away to cool his heels overnight in the cells. Olga packed his bags, left them on the front steps in the rain, and went off with the children to visit her sister, Kathleen, at the beach. Angelo removed his possessions from the deserted house. He did not try to return again to Olga. He was grateful to have been reminded of his limits. Unlike Olga, he knew the importance of accepting authority. She went her own way, would not bend; then let her be lonely and find comfort in that, if she could.

While Olga, so she decided, was glad to see the back of him. She was weary of men, their demands and their abuse. So it had been with her husband, so it was with Angelo.

THREE

IN THE SUMMER, WHEN SHE CAN FORGET the drips, the leaks, the damp, the cold, Olga is content to live with the bush.

Her asthma improves. She goes barefoot, feeling as light and energetic as the girl she once was on a South Island farm. She feels particularly light since Paul moved in. She calls him "our resident writer", and feels happy whenever she hears the diligent tapping of his typewriter. She and Paul are kindred spirits, Olga feels. She is restocking her paint tubes, one a week, out of his board money.

Olga stuffs a load of washing into the ancient washing machine, nicknamed Thrash and Bash, and scatters a cavalier dollop of soap powder. Beyond the cobwebby windowpane gleams a beautiful morning. She catches scents of jasmine, roses. Olga can breathe with impunity now that spring, her allergy season, has gone.

She leaves the washing to its own devices and wanders into the garden. It is there, it just has to be discerned. Olga knows where to look—pansies under the paspalum, geraniums in rusty tins, bulbs waving blooms like fists of triumph in unexpected corners. If there are weeds, surely weeds have a place. "Live and let live," says Olga often, and sincerely.

Somewhere back in the high grass the rooster is crowing. The bush fringe seems to have stepped back. It doesn't press in, as in winter, casting shadow and topping the lower arc of sunlight. The sky dominates in summer. Staring upwards, Olga tries to memorize that blue. She has a lot of trouble with skies. This week she will concoct subtler mixes with her new paints and experiment.

Childish wrangles from upstairs interrupt her. Humming to herself, Olga ducks her head to avoid the low door frame and pokes at the washing with the copper stick. Paul's striped pyjamas heave and disappear. It is a good feeling, having a young man about the place again—one so mild-tempered and polite, so manifestly grateful for Olga's small services. How happy she feels. Standing there at the tubs, she almost disappears. It feels like that. It's happened before; a severe attack of asthma can bring her to a similar point, as though she has left her body behind. Background sounds of animals, children, the heart-throb of ancient Thrash and Bash, recede. She stands, unselfed, just being in the fresh day. A sense of joy and peace stay with her even after she returns. She feels love for the world and whatever pervades and supersedes it.

"There's nothing for breakfast, Mum," Lilah shouts from the kitchen window. Olga just laughs. Lack challenges her. In no time she will create a meal where others see nothing but leftovers, scraps. "I'm coming." Olga smiles to think it's Thursday. Her mother taught her to wash, always and invariably, on Mondays, but Olga washes when the mood takes her. Even now she feels defiant, deliciously so, as she tops up the soap-suds and leaves the machine to pound its sluggish load.

Marian, next door, washes every day.
    She doesn't like dirt and she doesn't like smells. Particularly odours that lurk in concealed places. Better to pop the damp towels, the soiled underwear and shirts into the automatic every morning, on Half Load. That way she can keep control. Her washing's always out by nine a.m. She has a dryer but, weather permitting, she pegs out. Fresh air is free and deals with germs. Marian likes to compare the whiteness of her whites with Olga's subdued sheets and pillowslips. There are few enough moments in her day when she can confirm her usefulness in life. For Marian, a neighbour such as Olga is apt counterpoint. Olga is such a failure. Marian has lived next door long enough to have seen the comings and goings, the drunken husband, the violent boyfriend, the visits from Welfare. As well, she has an inside source of information. Dennis is a social worker and, while his area is closer to the city, he is in touch. Networks exist. Dennis has told Marian a thing or two. In strictest confidence. Marian hugs such knowledge close. When she feels restless and unfulfilled, it helps to remember Olga, and the awful mess some people make of their lives.

Dennis thinks Marian should be more charitable towards Olga.

Dennis believes his work has taught him to accept people as they are. Besides, being non-judgmental is an attribute of good counsellors. He tries not to overlook progress in his chosen field, just because he's middle-aged. He attends seminars sometimes, and tries to put into practice the techniques which visiting lecturers explain. He tries to make eye contact, to reflect, confront, and clarify. These skills do seem more effective than giving advice, an approach he noticed nobody ever took any notice of. If they now make changes in their lives his clients do so imperceptibly. At least, Dennis doesn't notice much difference. But they seem to like him more; fewer make a point of being out when he calls.

Dennis tried out the new skills on Marian. The lecturers warned that counselling techniques don't work in personal relationships. They were correct, it seems.

Paul on his mattress in the tower room hears breakfast sounds.

Olga bumps and bangs, Lilah is shouting, Steffie is beating with a spoon.

Paul reflects. Since he moved in to the pink house on the hill, he has begun three separate pieces of writing. There is the light magazine-style article, on being off work with hepatitis; and the paper for the laboratory file, on the procedure for the detection of *Pseudomonas Pisii* in commercially grown pea crops; and the short story about the break-up of a relationship between a sophisticated woman and a younger man. None of them is finished. Hepatitis seems to have eroded his concentration.

He stares at the ceiling and thinks of Linda. The last week has been better. He hasn't missed her so much, or felt so down. Perhaps his liver is responding to Olga's cooking, vegetarian quite often because she hates tracking into the village to buy meat.

Paul feels embraced by family life. Lilah sits on his knee and twines her arms around his neck. Olga listens to him, and laughs with him, and cheerfully irons his jeans, a task Linda declined.

Only Steffie twirls his stick, and doesn't look at Paul.

Children are playing in the park.

It is a joyful scene—grass, bright flower-beds, swings and slides. The bold ones climb to the top of the jungle gym and slide down the fireman's pole. The young teacher is kept busy fielding stragglers whom she sends back to the main group.

"On to the seesaw, Jason; roly-poly down the hill, Gary."

An old lady watches from the park seat. Short-sightedly she smiles. Summer and laughter. Such dear creatures, the little ones who play in parks on sunny days.

Helen checks her watch. She signals the children, pointing to the white minibus. Here they come, scrambling and clambering down the slope past the old lady; who stops smiling, who stands and hurries away from the children, away from the teacher who herself smiles, angrily.

"Into the bus, Steffie; hurry up, Mary."

The children are aboard, doors fastened, catches fixed. The white bus backs and turns, and the playground is empty.

The supervisor of the Special School hopes they will be back on time.

She has pushed the beanbags against the walls, swept up lunch crumbs, dusted the blackboard and put away the balls. She has to go to the dentist, also to the bank. Not a memorable afternoon. Never mind. Hers seldom are. The bus is back. Early. A full thirteen minutes to bell time, before the minibus can deliver its cargo home. Bother, Jessie thinks. It is like morning again without the refreshment of evening and sleep. How energetic, the way they run into the classroom; how keen the young teacher on their heels.

"No pushing, Gary; Shelley, wait your turn."

"How did they like the outing?" Jessie asks.

"Very much. They loved it, all of them, except the old lady on the park seat, who gathered up her coat in case they contaminated her, and went away."

Jessie understands. She never set out after tolerance but it has crept up on her. She makes no judgments of her children or the young teacher or the old lady. She knows there is no point. She sniffs. Her tooth aches. It makes her right nostril run. She wants to go home.

Helen plays music until bell time. The records are scratched, their dust jackets lost, and the player's even more dilapidated. The Seekers sing out. Round and round the pasting table the children stumble. Some sing loudly, some make strange noises. *"The CAR-nival is O-*

ver, I shall love you, till I die . . ." Helen can't help it, there are tears in her eyes, tears that they are so awkward and so ill-equipped. Of course she shouldn't feel sad unless she believed the world was the property of the bright and the beautiful—and who would endorse a belief like that?

"Come on, Steffie; join in with the others," Helen calls.

Stefan stays apart, twisting one leg around the other. Helen eyes him thoughtfully. She suspects he's out of place among these children. Each one of them has received a detailed history-taking and assessment, and their diagnosis is clear-cut. Microcephalic Gary, brain-damaged Jason, Mary the girl with Down's Syndrome. Nobody quite knows about Steffie. He doesn't speak, has rituals. Yet his I.Q. is probably normal. Well, they think it is. He won't join in with tests, either. As there has to be a diagnosis, his is written as *?autism*. Students who are visiting the school have Steffie introduced to them this way. "And here is Steffie. He is query autistic."

Helen wants further assessments for him; at least a visit to his home, liaison with the parents. She's said so to Jessie, who said, Hmm, possibly, but seems in no hurry to do anything. Jessie's an easy boss, Helen has to remind herself to offset her impatience. She may not take too seriously a young teacher pursuing new ideas, but she's taught Helen a lot. Jessie uses patience, touch, old-fashioned scolding, as any mother might.

Steffie won't sing but he likes the music, for suddenly he grins and runs outside to the swing. He stares down at the dull, scuffed dirt patch when he swings forward, and when he swings back he lets his head loll, and the cloud-images scud across his blue, opaque irises.

At bell-time the children collect their bags and the white minibus departs with its cargo. Jessie's red Morris follows up the driveway, and Helen locks up and hurries for her bus, not seeing her surroundings. Once she would have called herself "a country girl"; meaning, nature's beauty moved her. After all, that's why she took the flat in Titirangi. An impractical choice, such a poky little place, damp in winter, and main road traffic labouring up the hill outside her bedroom window till all hours. She never was practical. Dinah wasn't a practical decision, was born of the impulses of full moon and tide on a holiday beach in Rye, with assistance from a young man Helen discovered she didn't even care for in broad daylight.

Now she has the brisk walk of someone who must live by the clock. The bus bears her towards the peaceful hills but Helen doesn't notice. She is compiling one of her lists. Buy bread and eggs, pick up Dinah from the day-care, get the rubbish bagged and stapled. Last week dogs had a field day. After dinner, do some reading for the essay due at end of term: Saint Augustine, on Time. She's doing a Stage 1 Philosophy paper and, because of transport and baby-sitting problems, has missed several tutorials already.

She unlatches the child-proof gate of the day-care centre, coming out of her reverie. There's Dinah, cross-legged among the other children. The girl in charge looks embarrassed when she sees Helen—she is inspecting the children's heads for nits. It is routine, a precaution of proximity and hot weather, but some parents might take offence. Helen doesn't. She also carries out head inspections when parents are out of the way. "We recommend Lorexane," Helen says, by way of reassurance, "do you?"

The caretaker smiles. She wishes all parents were like this one. Dinah insists on fetching her satchel and shoes. At four, she is independent and growing, it seems, while Helen's back is turned. It is a pity, Helen thinks, that she has to be separated from her daughter while she earns their living in a setting almost identical, in terms of day-by-day activities. The swings and climbing frame look the same; yet Helen's not quite sure if she wants children like Jason and Steffie as Dinah's daily playmates. Feeling guilty, she decides, probably not. Waiting for Dinah, she remembers Steffie again. For two pins she'd take things into her own hands, call at his home unasked. He has a Titirangi address, can't live far away. A cautionary voice reminds her there are official ways of doing things. Helen sighs, then smiles as Dinah comes running and takes her hand.

Paul goes down for the mail.

He looks underneath the stone in the wooden crate which serves as a letter-box. There's a letter for Olga. Nothing for him. Well, the sickness benefit is only due tomorrow. The stamp on Olga's envelope is stuck on upside down. Paul takes a run at the slope and is hardly out of breath at the top.

Olga reads her letter warily. With letters from Kathleen, you never know, but her sister sounds quite normal. Summer visitors have taken over the beach. There's been a bit of trouble at the camping-ground—gangs, and broken bottles. Her garden's dry, but the watermelons are like footballs. She's well, and taking her medicine like a lamb, and pleased that Rowan's gone off nursing. A member of the family on either side of the mental health fence, so to speak. Olga should bring the young ones for a visit. She sends love.

Olga tells Paul that Kathleen has been prone to bouts of mental breakdown since adolescence. No apparent rhyme nor reason to them. Normal one day, back in hospital the next. Heredity, probably. Genetic tendencies could lie dormant for generations. Someone in the family tree is bound to have been batty. No disrespect to Kathleen, adds Olga. Paul agrees. His own family has produced a number of successes but he can't include himself among them. After all, he's only a lab technician and not too sold on that. There's nothing else he can do. He wants to write and yet. . . he gets started but it never shapes up. He must lack conviction, or talent.

Olga withdraws her hands from the sink and puts a soapy arm around his shoulders, dismissing his self-doubt. He can do it. She feels it in her bones. Some people are more sensitive than others. All her family are. Take poor Kathleen. You couldn't call her mad, not if you knew her. *Sensitive* describes her, as though she can't cope with the load of pretence you need to get through life. Paul knows what she means—those mechanical realities of conformity and routine which weigh one down. The ones like Kathleen are more honest. They seem to say, I can't be bothered with sanity if this is the way it requires me to live. Back to the hospital. It's a shame. Paul says yes; feeling understood. Together they lament the burden of a sensitive nature. Rainbows sparkle in the forgotten soapsuds.

Olga is looking through a recipe book.

Since Paul came, she has tried hard with meals. Only twice has she served curried lentils, her standby when all else fails. Olga decides on tuna pie, with a dash of curry powder for piquancy. *Buy tuna [2 tins]*, Olga scribbles on a scrap of paper which she props on the bench, so she can't fail to be reminded.

She sets up her easel. Today she will work again on sky. She can hear Paul typing in the tower room. His rhythm, now faltering, now steady, gives subtle encouragement to her brush. Paul in his tower, Olga at her easel. How companionable; fellow artists, alone yet somehow not apart. Paul's pace has picked up. He is in fine fettle by the sound of things. Olga mixes paint and adds a dash of violet for luck. She confronts yesterday's uncooperative swell of cumulus. Later Paul descends the ladder.

"Don't stop," he says, "I'll make us coffee."

Olga welcomes interruptions. She finishes with a swirl of cerulean blue, meant to suggest a wind current, and props her brush in turpentine. Paul fills the jug. Water spills on to the bench and soaks Olga's shopping list. While he waits for the water in the pot to boil he has a look in the food cupboard in case there is a packet of biscuits. There isn't. Paul has a little hoard, Chocolate Toffee Pops and Valencia Wafers, in his bedroom, but he doesn't bring them out in case Olga feels criticized in her providing. Paul likes to eat sweet things, alone and with a feeling of self-indulgence. His mother first, and Linda second, confirmed biscuits as undesirable. Paul carries in the cups. "Would you like me to knock up a letter-box?" he offers, shifting an upright chair into the sun. Olga's admiring look implies, Not only an artist, a craftsman to boot. Paul, who is avoiding a re-read of the unfinished draft of his serious short story, and who has spent the morning copy-typing the data on *Pseudomonas Pisii,* doesn't mind being admired. Olga's unremitting confidence in him is a new experience.

Olga says there is wood under the house and tools that once belonged to Angelo, whom she refers to as "my ex", much as another woman speaks of a former husband. Paul senses Angelo was more than a boarder to Olga. He doesn't like to pry, though he wants to find out more about her. She offers little information about her past as though, absorbed in broader histories, she feels her own to be of little consequence. She can make Paul feel absolved and free, accepting and dismissing his and Linda's differences with an airy wave, as though relationships exist, and cease to exist, and that's all that can be said. Paul enjoys her attitude. Sometimes after talking to Olga for a while about Linda he can imagine his short story converted to a comedy.

"You were typing nineteen to the dozen this morning," praises Olga. "The vibrations were inspired." Paul doesn't want to say he was typing a laboratory procedure. "It's hard to define exactly when one is working, and when one is not," he suggests. "Everything is grist."

They settle down to design a letter-box. It will have slots, and a sliding panel, and separate compartments for the letters and the milk bottles and the newspaper, which Olga never reads because she mistrusts reporters both historical and current. It will be painted by Olga, bright blue with impressionistic cirrus, and the number in yellow. Paul goes under the house in search of materials while Olga washes the coffee cups. She finds an ink-stained scrap of paper on the bench, scans it vaguely, and puts it in the rubbish sack. Paul returns with a few short planks, the worse for wear, and a rusty saw. Never mind, it is a start. Cheerfully he measures and marks. The short story can with justification wait for another day. Olga is very pleased about the letter-box. She stands by and entertains Paul, as she so often does. She has read so widely, and delved into so many topics of no practical use, that Paul's horizons expand, just listening. He allows a kind of grandeur in her contempt for reality as he understands it. Olga seems to free him from detail, to open him, to lure him on.

Dennis's area as a social worker includes the Special School.

He calls to check on Arthur, an amiable Polynesian boy under his care. Helen decides to ask his advice about Steffie. The white minibus has left and Jessie has gone home. Helen offers coffee. Dennis accepts. Conspiratorial silence seems to pervade the deserted building. Helen notices herself hushing the rattle of china as she sets out cups. The routine of institutions accounts for every minute, defines activity and role. There isn't a procedure for going behind the supervisor's back, nor for taking tea with the social worker after hours. Dennis ponders the insecure, somehow vulnerable way she puts her concern for Steffie to him. She seems to think the boy's a potentially normal child reacting to an abnormal environment. A suggestion like that has connotations of misdiagnosis, therefore awkward questions in official places.

"You have a *feeling* the child's not retarded? What *evidence,* exactly?" She resists the silencing note of authority, though already Dennis is reminding her of her inextricable place in systems, her powerlessness in life. It's strange, she thinks: he looks a kindly man.

"No *evidence.*"

"Better not be too precipitate, I feel. You make further assessments, I'll keep in touch. Now, may I offer you a lift?"

"No thanks." Though she knows her bus has gone. "I live in Titirangi—in the sticks."

Yet when Dennis says he does, too, she finds herself giving in; thinking, What's the use of fighting things?

Helen accepts a ride with Dennis.

Helen disappears through the gate of the day-care centre.

Dennis waits in the car, making entries in his diary. It has been an average day—office work, then two morning calls and four others after lunch. One client out, or conveying that impression. Arthur's family all sitting around the house, *Days of our Lives* on television, and the offer of tea, that ubiquitous social bridge. Arthur's family are doing all right. Dennis has been able to help them with a house and schooling for the slow son. He has organized a stay on the Health Inspector's decision in regard to inadequate sanitation, and has sorted out a legal infringement to do with cooking over an open fire in the back yard. Arthur and his family have presented satisfyingly solvable problems, and Dennis likes visiting them. They seem happy; a trait not too common in the lives of his clients, nor in his own life, come to that. Dennis has to deal with lack, outwardly manifesting as problems of money, work, health or housing. Yet he senses a more subtle dis-ease of frustrated hopes, disappointed human nature. Well, he's not exempt. His clients pick that up, for he's no steel-edged do-gooder. They can all sit down and share a cup of tea together and chat. He can help with a few of the practical problems.

Helen is pausing to latch the gate. A small girl clutching a paper banner follows her to the car and leans with composure against the sheepskin.

"I did a painting." She holds up the splotch of orange paint, which Dennis considers thoughtfully and from several angles. Dinah sits back satisfied.

Marian is waiting on the sunporch.

Dennis parks and walks towards her up the path.

Next door, the children are playing behind the overgrown hedge.

The shouts and laughter form a counterpoint to Marian's stillness.

She doesn't even wave to him.

He and Marian did try for children. A distasteful business of temperature graphs and semen analysis. Nothing really wrong, the doctor said, but still Marian hadn't become pregnant. Just something to accept, said Dennis, though it seemed a shame. Women might be softer, given babies.

"I'm home." An unnecessary statement, one would think, but Marian sits so still, hardly seeing him. Dennis lowers himself sighing into the chair beside her, narrowing his eyes against the setting sun.

Twenty years we've been married, Marian is thinking. That's a thousand weeks. Five thousand days, or seven if you counted weekends. She considers the next twenty years. Children's laughter penetrates the twilight like birdsong, until Olga's call is heard, and silence settles.

There is a scuffle near the hedge. The black hen is small and the rooster decisive. The hen stands surprised, shaking out its feathers. The rooster struts towards the porch.

"Disgusting thing." Marian emerges from her reverie, snatches the yard broom and descends the steps.

"I feel a failure sometimes," Dennis murmurs.

There is no contradiction from the garden.

Paul scowls.

He hates to fail.

It sounded a simple assignment. In the sketch it looked straightforward. The box is rebellious and rickety.

"I'll give it the undercoat tonight," suggests Olga, seeing Paul's downcast look.

"The timber's warped." Paul applies pressure at the joint to let Olga see and the side gives, a nail protruding through the split. "Fit it back together and put in more nails," Lilah advises, but Paul shakes his head.

"It's no good." He can't patch up so poor a job. Better an honest crate and a stone, than the falsehood of his carpentry. "I didn't learn woodwork at school," he adds unnecessarily.

"All great men make mistakes," cajoles Olga, turning up *The Blue Danube* on the radio. She's trying to get round him, he knows. And he can't resist. Her warm arm round his shoulder is a comfort and her teasing's gentle. He can't sulk for long. Lilah giggling behind them, Steffie peeping from his doorway, Paul forgets the letter-box and sweeps Olga round all the rooms in an impromptu waltz.

FOUR

At the hospital, Rowan is writing the nursing notes.

Her pen slows as she searches for exactness, as she crayoned at four, or translated French at fourteen. She likes afternoon shifts. At suppertime there is a smell of hot toast; and the night draws confidences from her patients. In a hospital like this there are no wounds to dress, no machines to X-ray misbehaving psyches. Talk is therapy. As a professional maxim, therefore, the gist of all talk is shared with other staff members.

Rowan is thoughtful as she recollects a conversation with Jerome, the school teacher who was transported to the hospital by the police after they picked him up naked on Jellicoe wharf. Jerome has made progress during the fortnight since his admission. He gets up now for meals and group therapy, where he says nothing. He knows they won't believe him. He has just told Rowan he isn't mad, merely under instructions from God, whose orders regarding his private baptism by immersion he was preparing to carry out when the police came along and interrupted him. Rowan is deciding how this information is to be transferred to the nursing notes and future staff. It worries her that she has been made to receive and become responsible for such information. Who is she to interpret the orders of God and the delusions of derangement? She has never experienced either. Who is to know how God speaks to man, or where a sense of spiritual mission overlaps with madness? There have been strange reversals of personality, magnificent overthrowings of the self, following God's reported appearance in the lives of men and women. Rowan, daughter of Olga, reflects on history's extremists. She wonders if history might have told another story if they'd had Melleril and the Mental Health Act back in the days of Saint Paul or Joan of Arc. As for Jerome, his behaviour in the ward has not been noticeably transcendent. He has stayed in bed and spent much of his time masturbating behind his cubicle curtains. But, thinks Rowan, who's to judge, who knows?

Her fellow trainees seem keen to classify—to come to grips with the predisposing factors, signs and symptoms, course, treatment and prognosis of the illnesses their patients exhibit. There are exams to pass. And it helps, when someone rages or turns a catatonic stare away, to know such conditions have a name and explanation. It is comforting to study Manic States or Depression, indexed under *M* or *D*. But Rowan sometimes forgets her patients are mad. A few psychotic people frighten her, and then she remembers. Yet she is used to odd moods, odd behaviour: her patients in their vagaries must compete with Olga, and Olga's family.

Jacob, Charge Nurse, has noticed Rowan's attitude. He likes her openness, her assumption that people can change. Yet he has worked in psychiatric hospitals for fifteen years, and understands their limits. Rowan seems like a mirror, reminding him of his own high hopes when first he came into the profession. He doesn't want to snuff out her enthusiasm; nor see her destroyed.

The middle road, that's Jacob's way.

Rowan's best friend is Josie, whose hair is red, whose language is crude.

Josie is not interested in the middle way. So far, life has returned to her a serious motor-cycle accident, a year in a Northland commune, affairs with Sandy and Pete, and an ectopic pregnancy which burst, causing Josie the loss of her right fallopian tube, and Josie's mother grief at her reduced prospects of grand-motherhood.

Josie makes her way with a limp and a humorous quirk to her red mouth. She is a good nurse. Rowan has seen her at work. She envies Josie's worldliness even as she can't help fearing the price of experience. Josie hasn't complained. She doesn't want pity and she won't feel sorry for her patients. They like her.

On their day off, Josie takes Rowan home for dinner. Mrs. Anderson is pleased Josie has a new friend, one who doesn't smoke or swear. Rowan is polite and offers to dry the dishes. She looks as though life has yet to reveal its underside to her, and she has never ruined her hair with acid green streaks. Mrs. Anderson, compulsively holding spoons up to the light, suggests to Rowan, "It is hard to be a teenager." It is harder to be a teenager's mother, reflects her distorted image.

She touches Rowan's shoulder, in sympathy towards herself. Josie too was once a lovely girl. Only, desired child, Josie. She is there, stored in the shoe-box, Mrs. Anderson's House of Memories . . . Josie in christening gown, Josie in her Plunket baby book, Josie on Santa's knee, Josie in her ballet *tutu*, Josie, flower-girl, Josie, marching girl. Josie, loved, late gift of destiny. Oh, what has happened to Josie?

Such painful hours to spend alone, Mr. Anderson shrugging off accountability, saying, They all go through it and grow out of it. Such a disappointment, not having quite come to grips with her own happiness, now watching Josie's slip through her grasp. Scouring the sink, Mrs. Anderson steals a glance at Rowan. She, a friend of Josie, seems normal. Could it have been nightmare, Josie's odd, aberrant period? Fantastic, far-fetched, like cups and saucers dancing in the moonlight or soapsuds frothing past waist, chest, mouth? "Josie has gone nursing," Mrs. Anderson tells her friends, and they all sound pleased. Yes, nightmare is the best explanation.

"Are you happy, dear?" she enquires of Rowan, for friends often do have things in common. The reply is obliterated by Josie's door-slamming entry, Josie's raucous laugh. She limps to the fridge, flings open the door, grasps a cold pork chop and gnaws with gusto.

"Hospital food stinks." Josie waves the bone towards her mother in a gesture of explanation. "Pig's-brain casserole and chicken-bum stew."

Mrs. Anderson smiles, a weak, capitulating smile.

She dries her cracked hands on the tea-towel and escapes to the bathroom. There, she stares at herself in the kindly lit mirror, remembering the happy, happy things that surely used to be.

Marian isn't happy.

Olga's rooster, joyously greeting the day, interrupts fragmented chases, searches, uphill pursuits. The rooms of Marian's dreams are solid and they have no windows.

Marian gets out of bed and looks in the mirror. Shadows stain her face as though an assault has been brought against her while she lay defenceless, dreaming. How tired I am, she thinks; perhaps I need a holiday.

For she needs something. Her life feels meaningless.

Marian goes to New Lynn and visits two travel agents.

They give her brochures to take home. She sits in the kitchen, reading about tropical resorts where crystal waters break on white sands, where people smile, and wait on you, and try to make you happy. She puts the brochures on the divider, where Dennis always looks for the daily mail.

She hears the school bus stop at Olga's house. It always comes at the same time. The service doesn't cost Olga a bean, she's sure. Funny how some people get everything for nothing—most likely because Dennis and the ones who work hard like him have to subsidise them.

There's Steffie running up the path, and Olga waiting, waving as she always does. Marian feels her breasts. She fills the kettle, sets out one cup and saucer and prepares a cup of tea. From her window she can see Olga's overgrown backyard, its tangled, useless fruit trees and its toppling chicken coop. Yet there are often visitors at Olga's place. And aging Olga, with her ugly clothes and her run-down house, has a young man come to live. It's odd, thinks Marian, pressing the warming cup between her hands—Olga is nothing to write home about.

At school, Steffie seems more withdrawn than ever.

As though he knows I'm watching, Helen thinks.

The sparkle of intelligence she has observed sometimes, coaxing him with books and counting games, is replaced with a stubborn, downcast gaze. When Dennis does call back to make enquiries, she feels foolish. There's nothing new to report.

"That's Steffie." She points him out to Dennis; Steffie on his favourite place, the swing, his head dangling down, feet scuffing in the dust.

"I know," answers Dennis, surprising her. "I've discovered he lives next door to me. Odd kiddie. Odd family. At least, my wife says so."

Helen is grateful for the lift home, and Dinah takes for granted this timely carriage come to transport the princess.

"My lunch was horrible," she announces, settling into the sheepskin seat cover.

"Did you throw it away?"

"I swapped it with my friend."

Dennis smiles at Helen, and pulls up outside the flat.

"You have to come in for tea," says Dinah firmly.

While Helen goes to the kitchen, Dennis looks around the small flat. There is a guitar, a scratched typewriter, piles of lecture notes, a doll's pram, folded washing, a television set, posters of the Greek Islands, curling at the edges. Helen brings a tray and Dinah settles with her toys, examining this large man who takes tea with her mother. She tips out her blocks with an approving crash and starts to build a wall around Dennis's feet, while he explains to Helen what his job entails. Dinah adds another level to the wall, and presses affectionately against his leg.

"I work the northwest side of the city," Dennis tells Helen, absent-mindedly moving his leg away from Dinah, "that's home visits as well as administration."

Dinah kicks the blocks over and goes running from the room. Dennis stares after her. It is the first personal message of need he has received in years. How desperate, that angry kick; how grave, Helen's eyes.

"She needs a father, I can't give that to her."

Inside Dennis, a gentle expansion of warmth. His maleness is wanted here. "I would like," he mentions carefully, "to drop in from time to time."

Helen says he may.

Paul isn't happy.

When the results of his recent blood and liver function tests came back, the doctor said, Excellent, and didn't offer to renew Paul's sickness benefit. He says there's no choice now: he'll have to go back to the laboratory.

"There's always choice," inveigles Olga, who hates to see him gloomy, "throw it in and be a rebel. Cap over the mill. Our family rebels go back at least to 1790."

It is cruel, the way Olga incites him to do the very thing he wants, and must not do. He can hardly bear the way she dangles great-great-grandfather before his eyes, like wine and meat before a shackled prisoner.

"His parents suggested the usual options—the Army, the Church or the Law. He liked the idea of Trade, no less. They were horrified, of course. No business man could remain their son. Out on his ear he went. He set up a coach-and-carrying enterprise from London to Bath and by all accounts did very well."

"What happened?" asks Paul suspiciously. Olga has been known to falsify the truth when fiction's ring is more robust.

"A minor catastrophe," Olga admits. "He went broke, through no fault of his own. Stevenson's *Rocket* ruined more men than my great-great-grandfather. The entire Canal System was scrapped—the steel and coal merchants saw to that."

"Well then." Paul is irritable. If only others would be practical, he might give rein to his desires. It's all very well for Olga, he thinks, drifting on her cotton clouds of fantasy. She'll be the first to grumble when there's no food in the cupboard for tea. Olga reads his mood and rests her small hand on his. "And there is your writing. How will you do it if you go back to that mundane round? Creativity is precious, we must take care of it."

"That may be, if one has a gift. But, Olga, we are amateurs. You've never sold a picture and I've never finished a story, much less been published. I have baskets of rubbish and you have landscapes propped all round the house. Let's not kid ourselves." Paul prefers painful truths to tact, but Olga doesn't take offence. She knows her painting is unoriginal. She presses his hand, offering him support. "You are feeling the weight of practical things. I know. I would happily waive the rent for you. We'd manage."

"Don't be silly." He feels comforted. Her faith in him is touching. She may be older, yet he feels the wiser of the two.

"I've nothing against money, of course, Paul. It's just I've never found a satisfying way to acquire it. Even if I had, I doubt I could have spared the time. It is the way I am."

"I know." Paul leans across and kisses her lightly on the cheek. "And thank you, Olga, anyway."

Paul returns to work.

His boss enquires after his health, not with noticeable warmth. Paul has been off work for more than two months and, because he is an efficient and unobtrusive worker, his absence has caused inconvenience. The temporary replacement acquired through the Department of Labour has been slow to learn and, in the process, has jammed the pea grinder seven times.

Rodney is very pleased to meet Paul. Now he can leave and he does so with alacrity, saying he hopes he never sets eye on another pea.

Paul looks around the laboratory. Rows of test-tubes line the benches. Pipettes, conical flasks and beakers stand in orderly lines. It is here that the search for *Pseudomonas Pisii* goes on. Before the sample peas can be processed, they must be ground into pea flour, and the grinding takes up the major part of Paul's working week. He will weigh out one kilogram of peas. He will turn on the pea grinder, a machine stored away from the main laboratory so that only Paul need experience its decibel level. He will collect the pea flour in a little bag, label it, wash the machine and swab it with alcohol, and repeat the process. By the end of the week he will have forty bags of pea flour. Each bag will be made into five litres of pea soup. Ten millilitres of this liquid will be removed by sterile pipette and placed in a sterile test-tube. One millilitre of this liquid will be placed in a sterile test-tube containing nine millilitres of sterile water, and a new solution will be made. A further millilitre of this solution will be transferred, sterilely, to a sterile test-tube containing nine millilitres of sterile water. One drop of this solution will be added to sterile broth agar. The forty test-tubes will be set aside over the weekend. On Monday, Paul will switch on the ultra-violet light and check the tubes. Given the nature of the job, he will feel elated if a glimmer of blue-green phosphorescence indicates Pea Blight infestation and financial ruin to some farmer. On Friday afternoon, Paul will do the washing-up of forty conical flasks, five litre; one hundred and twenty test-tubes, thirty ml; one hundred and twenty pipettes, one ml; eighty pipettes, ten ml.

Nothing has changed, thinks Paul.

It is all the same: only Paul has changed.

Chrysanthemums.

Shaggy yellows, prim-pleated mauves. Lovely, Helen thinks. On her way to a lecture, she is taking the steep climb through Albert Park. It was the leaving hour in Queen Street. No one smiled at her. She stared in the windows of book shops and boutiques. But it's April, Indian summer, in the park. On the grass, lovers lie and kiss, their arms encircled. The statue of Queen Victoria frowns down on two girls who sit holding hands: one, childish-looking in pink socks and ballet slippers, smiles trustingly, and turns to kiss her friend. Distantly a mower drones.

Helen stands and watches, as she might stand before a painting, waiting for its inner life to speak to her. Gulls, pigeons, painted park seats, the flowing fountain, girls in groups, their skirts spilling white and rose and blue banners on the emerald grass, all float suspended like watercolours on white paper. Helen has a sense of a changed reality, to do with the stillness, possibly, or the light.

A young man is chasing his little girl, who teasingly laughs, hiding by the fountain. His shabby jacket flaps as he runs past Helen, waving as he goes. She smiles, thinking of Dennis, who has promised to collect her after the lecture. He waits on purpose, although he claims office work as his reason, and she is glad she won't have to dash for the bus. As for any implications—well, they can be considered later.

Helen is running late. She hurries through the stone portals of the Old Arts building to her lecture.

A lecture by an eminent research scientist is to be held in the chemotherapy research laboratory after work.

A notice encouraging staff to attend has been circulated. Paul's boss arrives at the door of the room where Paul is grinding peas. Paul can't hear him. He shuts down the machine. As he feared, his boss assumes Paul will be at the meeting. Paul wants to say that *Steroid-related Stamina Trials on New-born Rats* is not one of his major priorities, but he has had two months off work, and the boss fixes him with a dour and unbeguiling eye, reminding him of the benefits of inservice education.

Paul nods and switches on the machine. His boss puts his hands to his ears, gives Paul a reproachful look, and leaves.

Paul sits near the back.

He is not pleased to be at the lecture. He is hungry, and wishes he were heading home to Olga and the family. He eyes the bald head and crumpled shirt of his boss with malevolence. To fear authority is weak; to bow to it in such scruffy form seems cowardly.

The scientist arrives with two wooden boxes and two buckets. He speaks for fifteen minutes on the endocrine functions of humans and rats. He discusses stress effects, and the interrelationships and deficiencies of hormonal compensation factors. He pins up graphs and scribbles formulae. He comments that the criticism of steroid therapy by untrained personnel who aim to discredit the scientist is completely without foundation. He proposes a simple experiment.

He brings forward one of the buckets, now seen to contain water. He opens a box and observes its contents with precision. These baby rats, he says, have been born to mothers untreated with steroids. He estimates their drowning time at two or three minutes, and certainly no more than five. His audience will see for themselves. He empties the contents of the box into the water and sets his stopwatch.

Paul sits and fidgets. It seems to him that his fellow workers look unnaturally alert and uncomfortable. The scientist presses the knob on his watch. A little under four minutes, he confirms, checking the bucket for signs of movement. Satisfied, he sets it to one side and brings forward the second bucket and box. These baby rats, whose mothers were steroid-treated, will display increased stamina, he suggests. In a stress situation, before they will succumb and drown, they will struggle for up to twenty minutes. He upends the squirming creatures into the water, resets his watch, and paces quietly.

One minute passes, and two, and three. The scientist checks the bucket, nodding to his audience. Paul suddenly stands up. He feels acutely embarrassed. He hates to be the centre of attention. He walks past rows of chairs towards the platform, and looks in the bucket, where a dozen frantic blobs flail about in the water. Paul picks up the bucket, pours its contents over the scientist's shoes, replaces the bucket, nods firmly to the scientist and departs.

Now he is five years old again, with a terrible urge to take to his heels. Being officially mature, he merely quickens his step. He reaches the bus stop unpursued by avenging angels. He starts to laugh. He's feeling very pleased with himself.

On her way to do the weekly shopping, Marian has had an accident.

She has run over the bantam cock. The soft yet somehow distinct resistance to her back tyre has set up a nasty apprehension; and sure enough, there he is, surprised beyond all hope, fine feathers not hiding the fact he's dead. Dead things give her the creeps. Dennis always sees to the mousetrap and takes care of foolish insects which mistake Marian's establishment for the Titirangi bush.

Marian fetches the rake. Trying not to look, she edges the rooster into the overhanging decency of the big flax bush beside the drive, and, with a sense of deep unease, drives to the shops. She wanders up and down supermarket aisles, trying to think about soaps and cut-price specials, but leaves without buying. The lunch she intended to treat herself to at the *Coffee Kiln* now seems unappetising. Feeling miserable, she drives home.

The flax bush has an evil presence; Marian realises she must confront the consequences of her accident. She finds a cardboard box and plenty of newspaper. With the help of a garden stake and the rake, she manages to put the rooster in the box and cover him up. Holding the carton well away, she goes to Olga's house, on the way practising what she will say if Olga is abusive. Marian feels guilty and slightly sick—she has often thought the bird belonged in the cooking pot, and said so to Dennis, yet she feels unjustly roped into the execution.

The new letter-box outside Twenty-five is very large, and painted bright blue with smudged white polka dots.

Paul cut the letter slot crooked, so that it seems to leer sideways at Marian as she edges past. Marian's expression does not change. A spotted blue monstrosity—it's what she would expect. Unsmiling, she conveys her cardboard coffin up the slope. Olga looks out and sees Marian climbing the path. Marian has something held forward like an offering. Of course people do bring offerings, cast-offs and windfalls, in boxes to Olga. There's Marian, she notes with surprise. Usually she acknowledges her neighbour much as she does the presence in her life of telegraph poles and other landmarks. Marian knocks and puts the box down on the step. She feels better with it off her hands. Olga greets her, beaming.

"I've run over your rooster." Facts are facts, no point in gentle words. "It's dead."

Olga looks confused. She crouches and lifts the newspaper.

"Oh dear," she says, "he certainly is."

"I thought you might want to cook it." Marian sees Olga's look. "Or bury it."

"He was a gallant chap," Olga says sadly. Marian feels nervous. Olga hasn't blamed her for her act. She stands uncomfortably while Olga gently strokes the lifeless creature. Marian feels appalled. Anything might happen now. Olga might nurse and rock the corpse, and clasp it to her breast, and show her incomprehensible sorrow in any kind of outburst. Death is bad enough, without emotion intruding—and all for a silly bird.

"I could ask my husband to come over after work and dig a hole." Olga replaces the newspaper. Marian can see one clawed foot, limp in death, and she tries not to shudder.

"If you like, I'll pay you." Though she feels obliged to offer Olga something, this, evidently, is not it.

"No," says Olga. "No thank you—no."

Marian feels reproached. She stares at Olga, thinking, Who does she think she is? They're poor as dirt.

Marian has run out of resources. She goes home.

Marian flicks through recipe books.

She enjoys cooking. She will try a new recipe on Dennis, who has been coming home late. He says they have increased his work load and reduced staff ceilings. How unfair, commented Marian, but he just shrugged, as though fairness has nothing to do with it. He's never been a demanding man. She can remember him coming into her life. Ten years older than herself, he showed her men could be gentle, could even welcome a young woman's powers of charm and fascination. So she married him: yet, oddly, having escaped home's dreary discipline, she felt re-engaged in battle, and a battle she had to win because in her heart she knew that power divided men and women. Unless you were on top of the power-heap you were at the bottom and ground down, as she'd seen her father crush her mother. Yet when

Dennis is away, as he is, increasingly, she wishes there were a way to start again on a happier footing, not having to prove he is weak, and she is strong.

Next door they are burying the rooster.

Marian watches from the kitchen window. The young man thrusts the spade with clean strokes while Olga holds the hand of the boy, the one who acts half mad. He can't seem to stand still, hops about like some leggy bird. The girl runs up with a bunch of flowers. Olga lifts up the cock, wrapped now in some kind of shawl, and places it in the grave. Paul replaces the earth. The child kneels and puts her flowers on the mound. They all stand silent, their solidarity reproaching Marian, who feels sad and alone. She had a hand in the death. It's not as though the rooster and Marian were strangers. The cock did ruin her garden and shatter her dreams. They were enemies, sworn and true. As enemies do, they needed each other.

Marian can't understand how Olga always gets away with things. What right has she, deprived and poverty-stricken and on the wrong side of forty, to that joyful little girl? To Paul, who mends her letter-box and buries her rooster; who, even as Marian watches, puts a comforting arm around Olga's shoulders? Marian remembers her last sight of the bird—his dead eye, his submissive slump in death. I'll be like that one day, she thinks.

Marian slashes at her tear, and slams the window shut.

Now the bantam rests in peace, crowned with pretty wildflowers, whom will Marian revile?

What is wrong with Waiheke Island? Dennis wants to know.

Marian seeks some place which guarantees happiness and inner peace. In the brochures, people tuck flowers in their hair and splash in warm oceans. It isn't like that on Waiheke. She's been there. The ferry made her sea-sick. The gulf wind cut as though it hated her. She didn't realise Oneroa and Little Oneroa were different bays, divided by a long and winding road, so she got off at the wrong stop and had to lug suitcases and then when she found the rented bach the beds were damp and rats played around the pit toilet and the whole time it rained.

As Marian reminds Dennis of these memories, he watches her and thinks her face is taking on a sharp and discontented stamp. With pleasure he recollects Helen's soft expression.

"Are you listening to me?" asks Marian.

"I'm listening." It is strange that Marian should look unhappy, when it is so long, he suspects, since he really hurt her with his words.

"So. You won't pay for me to go. Even on my own."

"It's impossible. The rates are due."

The rates are due. If there is also extra money put aside, that is earmarked. Dennis has seen a little bicycle with flyer wheels, just the size for Dinah. He isn't sure if Helen will accept—it could be seen as a claim. On the other hand, she might not mind, even if that's true.

Marian perceives her husband is thinking of something other than her holiday. "All right then," she says, "I'll get a job and pay for it myself."

She sounds bitter, not only towards Dennis. She feels no one will want to employ her. She's no good at anything—and even if she was, she has no way of proving it, and being paid as token of that proof.

Rowan has had a bad day.

The ward has been short-staffed, and Jacob brusque.

The new patient, Angela, has thrown her breakfast at Rowan.

The patients won't work in. They have to be chivvied and persuaded. Pamela huddles weeping, Robert feels a desire to eat compulsively, Phyllis has got hold of an old razor-blade and tried to scar her wrists. Rowan wants to discuss their problems with Jacob, but Jacob, sitting with Angela while she hallucinates in a sideroom, has no time for her. Rowan is dismissed to lunch.

She stares at congealing sausages, thinking how intimate it might be, Jacob and Rowan, in some discreet restaurant.

The ward is quiet when she returns. Angela is resting, and everyone else is at some group activity, or watching *Here's Lucy* in the recreation room. Canned laughter surges and fades. The only other nurse is watching television with the patients. Jacob goes to lunch.

Rowan adds comments to the nursing notes and answers a few phone calls. Some discordant undertone draws her to the corridor. Angela is crouched there, her eyes panic-stricken and unfocused. She starts to crawl away, scuttling as an animal might. As Rowan reaches her, she slithers full-length, along the linoleum, the tapes of her hospital gown parting to uncover her naked body. It seems stagey; a melodramatic imitation of madness. Rowan sets her fear aside and orders Angela to stand up and return to bed. She tries to help her up. Angela strikes hard, and Rowan tastes blood. As she shouts for help, Angela stands, trembling and powerful in her terror. She brushes Rowan aside and sways towards the exit door.

Rowan knows she's failed. Suddenly Jacob is there with the other nurse. Angela is carried and dragged to the side room where, sitting beside her, soothing her, forcing her to yield, Jacob slowly brings her back. At last she lies quietly and stares with passive eyes. Jacob waits, then beckons Rowan. She stays in the doorway. He goes to her.

"Let me see." He takes her hand away from her mouth.

"It's nothing," Rowan whispers, but Jacob eyes her with concern.

"All it needs is bathing," he says.

Rowan can feel his gentleness, and she covers her mouth again. Her own vulnerability has been brought home to her. She has felt inadequate and angry. She has been punched and kicked. She has watched Jacob press Angela's body and stroke her face and hair. She has waited for criticism and been given none.

"Go off duty. The afternoon staff will be here soon. Your lip needs attention. And you have had a fright?"

Rowan goes. She will burst into tears if she stays.

Jacob has spoken kindly to her, and touched her face.

FIVE

Indian summer fled, the park is just a place *en route* to somewhere else.
    Helen climbs the leafy path and people pass her walking down, heads bent, coats fast against the rain. Marigolds lie rooted out. The lawns are empty. The columned palms look lonely, sentries assigned point-duty, winter their watch. Helen fingers their age rings. She is writing her term essay. She considers Berkeley's argument that sensible qualities of objects are nothing but ideas in the mind.
    She leaves the trees and wanders, touching the wet park seat and the wire mesh of the litter basket. She regards the pool, its fountain stilled, its water the resting place of gulls in polar coats. She stoops and lets her

fingers enter the skin of the water, trying to discount conditioned expectations. Cold and wet, the water communicates itself as she knew it has to be. Yet Berkeley expects her to accept the water's wetness as an idea, to believe its coldness has no objective measure . . . even that the water, following his further proposition that physical objects are no more than their sensible qualities, isn't there at all.

The lecturer has challenged his students with that possibility, slamming his hand on the desk and defying one of them to prove its existence. Helen was confused. She had expected philosophy to provide knowledge— that was why she enrolled to attend two lectures and a tutorial every week. So far, her knowledge hasn't increased and her certainties have been turned upside down. Now she hardly knows what she knows, much less what she doesn't. It's confusing. Intelligence has always seemed a gift, and reason a gracious attribute. She has to wonder at educated people who imply she can walk through walls if she changes her perception of the material world. She suspects a game, for surely they don't believe themselves. Yet she's intrigued. The world does feel more mysterious. The water opens for her hand; she wonders what else its parting might signify.

Droplets separate out and hang from her fingertips. She watches as they yield their independent form and fall, re-entering the body of the pool.

Olga is at Paul, persuading him to be true to himself. She applauds his tale about the rats. It's a good story. Paul thinks so, even after he is summoned to the head chemist's office and informed his recent record of attendance and attitude leaves much to be desired. Work like his calls for stability and application—qualities many unemployed technicians wait eagerly to demonstrate.

Paul feels acutely conscious of the nudges of threat and manipulation his boss adopts to keep his staff subservient. His independence hardens. Olga has faith in him. Her source of belief, fed by centuries of age-old power struggles against authority, in turn flows in to him. He hands in his notice then and there.

Olga applauds and cooks a special dinner. Paul buys the *Star* and starts to search the *Situations Vacant* columns. He needs a job which occupies the body and allows the mind to receive ideas.

"I want ideas, Olga."

Olga understands. Outdoor work is good for the soul, she says.

"They want a keeper for the golf course. That's no good, I've never kept a green."

"Say you have." His honesty is admirable but Olga doubts it will land him a job.

"A builder's labourer? I wouldn't be much good at that."

"You made a splendid letter-box."

"It's still standing, that's the most you can say for it."

"You are too critical, Paul." Her body brushes his as she reads over his shoulder. Light as a moth, he thinks; hard to realise she's made of normal flesh and bone. "There! The very thing, a nursery-man."

"But I hate gardening."

"How do you know?"

"I was paid when I was a kid, to squash white butterflies."

"Enough to put anyone off. I believe you'd make a gardener. It does things for a man, working with nature."

"What does it do?" Sometimes he could lift her off her feet and spin her like a little girl, she is so fanciful.

"Lawrence knew. And Lady Chatterley found out."

Paul laughs out loud, and so does Olga.

Helen is waiting for Dennis outside the university.

When his car pulls up she dashes through the rain and settles thankfully against the sheepskin. He often seems to be there when she is most likely to accept. What harm in going home with him? He so obviously prefers her company to his wife's—one of those suburban housewives, she presumes, caught up in her routines. All the same, she feels guilty. She must sort out just what their friendship means. She will, soon, when the holidays start and she can stay home with Dinah after school and watch *Metal Mickey* on TV, instead of going all the way to the city in search of understanding.

Rowan is home for her day off.

She says she has a test to study for, and takes her textbooks silently away. She lies on the spare bed, the rug pulled over her. Olga, in the doorway, eyes her eldest daughter with concern. She suspects the hospital of nefarious demands. She accepts that children must grow up and move away. But she misses Rowan, who comes home only once or twice a month, and with a withdrawn manner that suggests to Olga, Keep away.

"You're not studying? What happened to your lip? Did you have an accident?"

"Nothing happened." Touchy Rowan pulls the tartan rug more firmly round her face. "Of course I'm not studying. How can I, when it's freezing cold and there are people everywhere?"

It can't be helped, that there is no coal, no wood; that Steffie's home with a cold and Paul is out of work; that Olga's boudoir, where Rowan might have crept to feel a little girl again, protected from the world's harshness, is at present a sorting depot for the cards and newspaper cuttings and velvet scraps Olga's collecting since she is trying her hand at *collage*.

Rowan is tired, and tired of neurotic, crazy people who expect her to absorb their madness and sadness. She's too old to ask for hot Ovaltine and a story. That was one kind of love and she hasn't found a replacement. Jacob doesn't care, and she can't run to Olga anymore.

"I want to get some sleep. Please tell Paul not to whistle. And I hope it's not curry for tea."

Cold Rowan shivers pointedly and turns her back on Olga.

Lilah brings a letter for Olga, who paces, flushed.

"Uniforms!" cries Olga, holding the offensive page at arm's length. Paul takes it and reads it. Olga is reminded the school gave notice at the beginning of the year that gym uniforms were required, and that Lilah is now the only child in her class who continues to participate in ordinary dress. The teacher invites Olga along for an informal chat, and mentions that in special circumstances spare outfits can be provided free.

"A reasonable letter," Paul suggests carefully.

"Reasonable? Officialdom!"

"They just want her to wear a uniform like the others."

"Exactly! How humans love uniformity! I shall remove Lilah from school."

"You can't," says Paul. "You have to provide alternative education."

"I don't want to be removed." Lilah sounds upset. Her mother might be cajoled, but this impassioned empress is another matter.

"I shall take you to the country. Your individuality will be crushed before it ever has a chance to flower."

"I wore uniforms, Olga. I didn't mind."

"And look at you!" Olga glares, and Paul decides she's rather magnificent when she's angry.

"What about me?"

"You are warped."

"I am not."

"Of course you are! Take your creativity—bruised, smothered."

"Thank you, Olga."

"You don't know what I know. I know bureaucrats."

Lilah raises her voice. "I hate the country! And I'm getting a part in the play."

"We shall find some far-off place, away from rulemongers. We could go to a lighthouse."

"Too isolated."

"The perfect retreat for a writer."

"Olga," Paul says patiently, "I'm not a writer."

"What rubbish! A writer by intent . . . Oh, we could live as we liked on a lighthouse. I know Morse. We studied it when we all had English measles. We had to darken the rooms, but we had our torches and the Columbia Encyclopedia."

"You must be the only person in the world who could turn the English measles into a teaching session and an adventure."

"I am a born teacher, that's why."

"You are. You teach me constantly and in the most entertaining way. But we're not going to a lighthouse."

"They won't make conformists of my children!"

Close to tears, Lilah runs to Paul and flings her arms around his waist. "I don't want to go to a lighthouse. I like uniforms. Everybody wears them."

Olga shudders. "It's happened already."

"Lilah really does have a point, you know." Paul wonders whether Olga, devil's advocate for the *status quo*, can allow others a more peaceful course.

"Be moulded as you please," snaps Olga, pacing, "but I believe society must be shaped by the people, not the other way round."

"Olga the revolutionary? I've heard you say that violence breeds violence."

"It does." Olga sits down. "It does."

"Go and talk to the teacher," suggests Paul gently, "he sounds reasonable."

"No." She looks uncertain, and Paul senses that, to be herself, she needs the safety of her private world. In that outer organisation of work and material fulfilment, she is merely middle-aged and shabby, a poor, eccentric woman at odds with everybody. Olga knows, and refuses to be judged.

"If you like, I will go."

Olga looks grateful. "Thank you. You are quite likely right. It might be a good thing, if someone went."

Rowan, plucked from sleep, lies and listens.

Even in disagreement Olga and Paul sound friendly. A long time ago, there were other fights, true adult hates and angers. This is some simple matter to do with uniforms.

She lies in the dim light, feeling drowsy, feeling a little girl again without responsibility. Olga made Rowan's choices then—took her away from the convent and sent her to the state school . . .

Mass on Sundays. Rowan would find a clean dress and hunt up a pair of sandals and try to plait her hair neatly. She made her own breakfast, since Olga didn't go. The cats rubbed round her ankles, wanting scraps, and she felt grown up, deciding. She had to be outside the Bannisters' gate by eight-thirty. Not a minute later, Mary said. Mary was their daughter. Rowan didn't like her much, but because they went to the convent together, and came home together, they usually played together at lunch time. There was always a nun on playground duty, pacing with her hands tucked in her long sleeves, but there were a few quiet places the nuns overlooked. It was like that in the grotto, where the Saint's statue stood in its niche.

"Let's pick flowers for the grotto."

"That's stealing." Rowan knew Mary was wrong. When you picked flowers it made way for more, but Mary said, "You'll go to Hell." She knew all about Hell, where it was, who went there, how hot the fire was. Mary was a know-all.

"I don't believe in Hell."

"That's a sin."

"I don't care." Rowan did, though. She'd been taught about good and bad but it was all mixed up since Dad went off with Isobel. He'd done a bad thing. People looked sorry for their family and brought them old clothes. But when she'd seen Isobel run into the rain to kiss him, she'd thought Dad was sensible to pick Isobel instead of Olga.

Olga never kissed Dad, in the rain or out of it. And there weren't fights, with him gone. Olga and the kids would curl up under blankets and the cats would purr. Waiting for Dad to come home, there'd been a not knowing, and Steffie would grizzle, and Olga would look cross, and Rowan would worry and not feel like eating her dinner. It was better without Dad.

"Let's play Saints," said Mary. Rowan didn't know how to. Mary said to kneel down and say prayers, so they knelt on the hard ground and whispered holy things to God.

"It's not much fun," said Rowan.

"Saints do other things," said Mary. "They sleep on boards and beat themselves."

"What for?" Rowan was interested. She would like to be a saint, but she said a nurse, if people asked.

"So they won't go to Hell, stupid. Do you want to play?" Mary picked up some twigs. "Here's my scourge, does it hurt?"

"I can't feel it."

"Saints take their clothes off," said Mary. So Rowan stripped off her tunic and blouse, and Mary tried the twigs again.

"Don't do it hard! It's horrible!"

"You should do it for God." But Rowan knew it wasn't for God. She felt funny, fluttery inside. Soon she had a turn.

"Am I bleeding?" Mary tried to get away and Rowan chased her. Trying to get in as many smacks as Mary had dealt Rowan, she bumped into Sister Felicity, come to check which disobedient children were out-of-bounds. They were marched to the head nun. They tried to explain about being saints but it did no good.

"Mary Bannister," the head nun said, "a Catholic child from a Catholic home and this is the behaviour of you!" Then she turned her eyes to Rowan, a convert, and said, "As for you, Miss, your mother will be hearing from me."

Olga was informed her daughter had instigated unhealthy

and immodest practices among the other children. The convent was distressed. Olga was furious. The Church of Rome was inhabited by hypocrites, she said. She withdrew Rowan to a state school, and herself from the Church.
Rowan missed the convent. She had liked the little chapel, its statues and incense and the daily lessons in religion. Olga let her go to Sunday School instead. It was better than having to kneel up straight or sit still during endless sermons. But she knew the sticker prizes and Bible stories and free picnic each year didn't have much to do with God. Whenever she passed the convent she looked away. The sight made her feel an outsider—someone not good enough.

The sound of chopping wakes her.

Paul is outside, taking firewood from the peach tree's dead branches. Its winter skeleton clatters on the windowpane as Paul works. The sky behind the tree is dull.

She yawns and gets out of bed. She doesn't care about the test or the hospital. Her roots are here in this shabby repository of all her life's living. Here, people love her—Olga, and the kids—maybe even Paul would if she gave him some encouragement. He certainly likes it here. He looks different, more relaxed. He might be good to talk to.

Wrapped in the tartan rug, she slouches to the sitting room. The fire crackles, and she can smell the scones Olga has just lifted from the oven. Lilah, sprawled on her stomach, is crayoning. Curled in the frayed cane chair, Steffie is staring at the flames. Rowan yawns and yawns. It would be so good to stay like this, warm in the red rug, the fire sparking, butter melting on hot scones, fresh tea steaming in one of the best cups. Steffie is delighted she's home. His little smile sketches pleasure on his solemn face. He goes back to staring at the fire. Rowan imagines his dreams—fire-spitting dragons or bush birds free and soaring as the flames mount, sacrificing earthly form in that fierce rush to liberation?

Paul is going out to buy a newspaper.

He pauses at the door and signals Steffie, for, thinking about it, he's not seen Steffie taken anywhere, except by special bus to school. Olga guards him closely. Now she appears at the kitchen doorway as though warned by some psychic sense.

"I think not, Paul; he has a heavy cold." It is as though she has placed a possessive arm around her only son.

"A walk might clear his head."

"He has a cold."

Steffie looks from Olga to Paul.

Olga loves Steffie intensely, protectively. Paul realises how she can bind people with the silken strings of love.

"All the same," he persists, "I will take him out soon; when the cold is better. Meanwhile I shall invite Rowan instead." He smiles as she pulls the blanket closer, yawning, and he goes to her. He reaches under the rug, finds her hands, pulls her up. "Come on, lazy."

"Oh," she protests, "why should I?"

"Please? Because I want you to."

Rowan lets him pull her to her feet, feeling shy, for his hands are strong. She could never introduce a conversation about love with him. It would never do. She racks her brains and asks instead, "What happened to your lab job?"

"I left."

"That must be nice." She sounds wistful. "But why?"

Put like that, Paul's not sure. Cap over the mill. It's all very well. Now he has no work.

He delivers a careful lecture on completing challenges one has set for oneself, expecting Rowan to laugh, as Olga would. Instead she listens attentively, as though his advice carries an older man's weight, a father's authority.

It hasn't been much of a day, decides Dennis.

The police apprehended a child from one of the families on his file, and Dennis had to deal with it. He's been to the police station to sort out the situation as best he can. He thinks of the mother, a woman not mad enough to be committed to a mental hospital, who bars her door and keeps her children hostage from the dangerous world. The boy has given Dennis's name as his only friend. Dennis has returned him to his home and cautioned both mother and son on the truancy laws.

Driving home, he is thoughtful. His job can seem a confirmation of his ineffectiveness. Often his clients live in rented rooms where a one-bar heater burns in winter and soap operas play all day long. He can't help much. He can listen to the problems, make the odd suggestion. Perhaps that's of some value. He wouldn't mind someone like that to visit him and listen, as he must, to the recital of frustration. His own life isn't stunning. Is it his work? If he had a different job, in entertainment or travel . . . but that reminds him of Marian, who leaves tourist pamphlets in his sock drawer and insists that he is mean. Wednesdays are better, when he collects Helen and plays with Dinah and relaxes a while before going home to Marian. But Helen doesn't want his services tonight. She said she had an extra lecture. Dennis wonders.

"You're home early." His wife can make it into an accusation. Dennis makes his own coffee.

"We're out of milk."

"Then put the bottles out yourself." I'm not your slave, her tone implies. Well, Dennis didn't think she was. Silent, he searches for small change.

Always into his own thoughts, reflects Marian. You don't know what goes on in people's heads—or bedrooms.

"*She's* got a new boyfriend." Marian nods in the direction of Olga's house. "Pushing fifty, I'd say, you'd wonder what they see in her."

Dennis is nearing fifty. He remembers that Helen will turn thirty in October, and he looks coldly at Marian.

"You shouldn't judge people."

"Why not? You are judging me."

He nods. She is right.

At six o'clock Helen walks through the portals of the university. Summer's friendly idleness has gone. Motorbikes roar purposefully, their owners in a hurry for home and hot dinner. Helen sets out for the bus stop. Dennis won't be there tonight. All the same, she scans parked cars as she battles wind and rain. The chill air makes her ears ache.

Her facade of independence is easily undermined. At the pedestrian crossing a group of bikies, threatening in the surreal illumination of street lamps, eye her and shout propositions. Haughty, she stares past them, feeling needy and afraid. Not waiting for the signal to cross, she makes a dash for the bus, and takes the dark ride back to Titirangi.

SIX

ABOVE OLGA'S BED IS A PORTRAIT of Julia, her grandmother. Shoulder-length black ringlets frame her gentle face. Her gown, the kind a well-to-do Victorian woman would choose, is scooped upon a tender neck. Julia must like the room she oversees. She looks out serenely as though to say, Don't fret, nothing is permanent. She was twenty-five when she sat for this painting. She died two years later, of diphtheria. Olga keeps track of such details. She keeps her ancestors alive, their goods in trust. Most of the furniture in the room belongs to Julia; that is why her treasures are in Olga's boudoir, safe from cats' claws and the children's rough-and-tumble.

There is her oil lamp on the davenport, and the rose-patterned china bowl and ewer on the walnut stand. Julia's hand-made garments are wrapped in tissue paper in the wardrobe drawer—drawn-thread chemises, pin-tucked night dresses, each initialed in embroidery. When Olga's parents died, and the relatives dealing with the estate enquired of Olga what she wanted, she wrote and asked for Julia's things. They said among themselves how odd it was that she would want yellowed underwear and oil lamps when, with those poor children and no money to her name, she surely had more need of cutlery and blankets. They gave her what she wanted, as Olga knew they would; her reputation within family circles being more equivocal than her sister's—Kathleen was at least officially mad. Olga received her treasures from the carrier, who staggered up and down the hilly track with the spinet and chaise longue, avoiding the rotten porch boards which Olga pointed out to him. She arranged the furniture, set out the silver-backed brushes, and hung Julia's portrait as though establishing an honoured guest. Her ancestors reassure Olga that the demarcations of birth and death are only gentle gear-shifts in a larger scheme.

Olga has made a point of studying the reverent attitudes so many cultures display towards their dead, and has seen how within her own civilization the belief in continuity has been eroded. She finds it easier to accept life's random surprises, knowing that, but for Stephenson's *Rocket* and the failure of great-great-grandfather's carrying business from London to Bath, he might never have encouraged his son to emigrate to New Zealand. Great-grandfather, in 1862, mightn't have embarked on the *Hanover,* disembarked three months later at Auckland, gone into land development, and six years afterwards married Sarah Trounson. Grandmother Julia might never have been conceived and born and been instructed in the arts of water-colouring and needlepoint, nor learned to play the harp, nor met and married the bright young barrister Edward Jervis. At twenty-six she mightn't have given birth to premature Robert, nor died just one year later of diphtheria. The puny baby might not have grown into the six-foot-tall man in love with land, and with an enterprising eye that surely related back to 1792 and the birth of great-great-grandfather himself. He mightn't have taken Hester Carmichael to wife, nor begotten several more children in the family succession, including Olga: who, in the unpredictable course of things presently occupies a pink house on a hill, and there erects the family tree and teaches her own children their place within it.

The gentle flow of time feels right to Olga. Dreamily pushing the vacuum cleaner's suction head to and fro on the lovely, faded carpet, she decides the world is in too much of a hurry now. In the thick of the jet age she has hardly come to terms with the hydrogen balloon. Machines play unkind tricks on her. The fridge and the washing machine threaten collapse. As for the vacuum, its wheeze becomes a high-pitched whine and Olga sees a spark. She sniffs, thinking of fire and the phoenix. The burning ghats by the Ganges would surely have a symbolism quite absent from Western cremation procedures—the one celebrating human passage in the vitality of leaping flame, the other automated and sterile. Surely people have lost their bearings in the West. Symbols are scorned, a sense of awe has died. Olga hoovers vaguely round the legs of Julia's writing desk. One of them was fractured years ago by Angelo in one of his drunken tempers, and mended amateurishly. The crack still shows. Poor long-gone Angelo. Olga can hardly remember him, except for such promptings. Olga has forgiven him any damage he did, though surely at the time she would have been upset, destruction of Julia's furniture being of more account than any assault on Olga herself.

A short explosion suggests the vacuum cleaner has expired. Olga checks the light switch, hoping there is a power-cut, but there is no power-cut. She sighs, turning to Julia, her expression seeming to say, Surely I am in the wrong time, or place? Grandmother gazes upon her as though her doubts have been heard and understood, and Olga feels comforted. In other settings a woman may take offerings of oil and flowers to her ancestors' shrines, so they may accept her tokens and, with them, her place in their line. Feeling that urge, Olga steps over the vacuum cleaner and sits before the dressing table. Shaking out her plait, she takes up one of Julia's silver-backed brushes. Brushing her hair, she imagines herself in a time of jolting rides on rutted bullock-tracks. Threshings, burn-offs, the felling of bush; a smithy anvil ringing, wedges clinking, the mill-saw running; orchard fruit-gatherings and Sunday picnics, the women in their full, high-buttoned gowns and wide-brimmed hats; flash-flood, storm, private feuding, public warring, birth, sickness, burial in a quiet plot beside a white-painted wooden church.

Julia must have sat like that at night, brushing out her beautiful black ringlets by lamp light. Her serene regard speaks to Olga, telling her, Believe your intuition; there is a link between us, the link of our lineage, the link between the living and the dead.

Olga goes down for the mail, finding advantage in the death of the cleaner after all.

Housework can always be done later. The sun is shining and the benefit cheque has arrived. Olga feels her spirits lifting. There are two other letters, neither one a bill. The ginger cat suns itself in the milk compartment, its white neck ruff standing out in a proprietary manner. How clever Paul is, says Olga to the cat, stroking its chin; his letter-box is excellent, is it not?

Checking the bus timetable, Olga stuffs the day's mail in her purse, puts a safety-pin in her skirt, and takes herself quickly up the road. Halfway to the bus shelter she remembers she has left the front door open. Never mind, it is too late to worry now. If a visitor or tramp comes by, why, they can always make a cup of tea and come back later, if the matter is an urgent one.

The Post Office is crowded, always is on Benefit day.

Olga can wait. She lets people push in if they want to. They may be in more of a hurry than she is. Olga hitches at her waistband where the pin is digging in, and looks around. Olga may sport a pin or two, but the woman ahead looks like a well-strapped parcel, with a baby slung in a carrier on her back, one toddler fighting leather reins and another escaping altogether to climb and scribble all over the deposit slips. The mother moves forward, yanking on the reins. She looks worn out. Olga's not a fool, she can well remember her own tough patches, with bare cupboards, a heavy heart, no one to go to for sympathy.

Olga tries to make the baby smile. She loves children, always has. She knows they grow and leave. Now Rowan comes home withdrawn, as though her mother conspires against her. Olga has tried to talk to Paul about Rowan, but he is reading psychology and she has no patience with such fiddle faddle. Paul means well, of course, but she has to laugh at his ideas. Daughters disowning their female models for a time, in order to become themselves? It's the kind of thing Freud and his band made capital of, writing their gospel for twentieth-century neurotics, but Olga has no time for it. Paul offers her books which she returns unopened. No psychologist will dictate to her the latest crack-pot theory that will soon be as dated as last week's news. Olga has tried to share her own belief that loyalties stem from the past, from family and origins. She reminds Paul how the Nepalese offer flowers and rice-cake, the Orientals make shrines, the Gilbertese annoint and revere the ancestral skulls, because they understand the basis of security. All Paul will do is smile and say, Yes, yes; but is it after all so different, Olga searching the external past, Rowan unravelling the inner?—until Olga wishes he would pack up his theories and go back to his writing, which is what he is supposed to be doing.

The queue shifts forward. The baby's skin, how tender! There is much that puzzles Olga. She has always thought of children as a gift. Modern attitudes seem to her to view them as a punishment. No doubt it is to do with materialism—roller-skates, holidays, fancy clothes. Rowan never complained about going to school barefoot, or wearing hand-me-downs. If there were requests Olga had to turn down through lack of money, surely she made up for them in other ways? That episode when all the rest of Rowan's class went on a ski weekend to Mount Ruapehu, and Rowan had to stay behind . . . yet Rowan understood, surely? It has all become too elaborate, too ambitious; when Olga was small she was quite happy to toboggan down grass slopes in a cardboard box.

At least Paul has brought home a good report from Lilah's teacher, who describes Lilah as gifted at art and acting, and academic if her potential can be brought out. Olga knows all about that. Let well alone. What's genuine will out, in spite of theorists always keen to experiment on a new generation of guinea pigs, and then write papers on what went wrong. Olga could do the job with never a ski trip nor a school uniform entering the picture.

Steffie—she can guess his rating in the modern coin. Let the world despise the weak, but not when Olga's there to act as shield. Anyone who interferes with Steffie will see a side of her to reckon with.

The teller stamps her benefit cheque and crisply snaps the notes. Olga thanks him graciously, as though the gift is personal. Benefit day, it is a little festival. Old books and records sell for a song at the Op. Shop. Olga stuffs the money in her old brown bag. Plait bouncing, she goes out to celebrate the day.

Paul feels his day has been productive.

He has been to the Special School and spoken with Helen, Steffie's teacher, and has found himself a job with a Danish market gardener. The Dane has demonstrated how to cut and strip the cabbages and pack them for the market. He has told Paul to start on Monday, and given him an enormous cabbage to take home.

When Paul arrives at the Special School, carrying his cabbage, Helen is on hands and knees, collecting packets from the play grocery shop where the children learn to buy and pay for food. Looking over her shoulder, she sees a head of fair, curly hair, a checked cap and a cabbage assemble into Paul, who says hello, he'd like a word with Steffie's teacher. Helen scrambles to her feet, brushing dribbles of soap powder from her skirt, and invites him into the office where the files are. Paul wants to know more about Steffie's handicap. It's not clearcut, says Helen, handing Paul the file.

Reduced to typed paragraphs of clinical assessment, Steffie sounds like someone else—a problem personality, lacking in the social graces. They probably mean he scratches his balls in public, where I do it privately, Paul decides. He doesn't say so to Helen. Instead he asks the official definition of 'anti-social', and Helen wryly shakes her head. No one seems to understand what's wrong with Steffie. He's not unintelligent. Helen thinks he perceives far more than he lets others know. He is a puzzle. She would like to see how he reacts at home.

Paul nods and invites her to visit. Meanwhile he could provide social experiences—a train ride, a visit to a soccer match, walks around the district.

Helen thinks that is an excellent idea.

Olga has had a good day, too.

For Lilah she has paints and a track suit, for Steffie Roman sandals and a xylophone, for Rowan a flowery summer hat, for Paul striped braces, not a trace of wear in the track suit, everything a bargain, enough in hand to feed them handsomely for the rest of the week.

"Paul's brought home the biggest cabbage in the world," announces Lilah, and Olga takes it, laughing at nature's whimsy, and gives Paul his red and yellow striped braces. He clips them on and tips his cap. Claiming the cabbage, he does a little tap-dance with it, so that Olga giggles, and murmurs, "Ah, Paul—mon charmant bouffon!"

It rains, the first week of Paul's new job.

The Dane lends him an old oilskin but the water trickles through. Soon his sandshoes are sopping, and his jean cuffs. After the first hour his knees and his back hurt. He wipes the rain from his eyes and looks along the rows of cabbages, hundreds mutely sprouting all the way to the horizon. Paul bends his back again. It was easier working in the laboratory.

Later the sky lightens and birds explode in trim formations from the wind-breaks. Clouds crack open and the sun bursts through, making the wet cabbage hearts pulse with life.

From the window, Olga can see Steffie, bouncing beside Paul.

She steps back in case they turn and see her, like an unwanted portrait propped there in the attic. But Paul doesn't look back. His work's cut out to keep pace with Steffie's grasshopper leaps and side-steps. Steffie tugs at the knitted cap which Olga jabbed with unaccustomed roughness on his head. He hops to one side of the ditch and then the other. He finds a soft-drink can tab and picks it up. He fingers it, pokes his tongue into the hole and runs fast like that, his tongue out, folded into a tube along which the wind can trickle. The power pylon seems to excite him. He stops, hops, touches it, licks it. He finds a hole and puts his face up close and peers through and starts to laugh. He waggles the can-tab at Paul.

"Put your tongue in," Paul says. "People will think you are a half-wit if you run about with it sticking out." Steffie puts his tongue in. Paul can see he doesn't want to wear the hat. "Take it off, then," he says, for it does make Steffie look silly—a green and yellow crocheted hat stuffed like a teacosy on his head. Steffie gives the hat to Paul, who puts it in his jacket pocket. Steffie's ears stick out, red, tender-looking.

"Which way?" Paul asks at the main road junction.

Steffie goes left.

"That's the filter station, and those are storage ponds. Titirangi stores water for the city because we get more rain than most places. The water has chemicals added to make it safe to drink. Those flowers, they're called ranunculi, and those are polyanthuses. My new job is cutting cabbages. I'll show you one day, if you like. Let's run—if you beat me, I'll buy you a treat at the dairy . . ."

Are you listening, Steffie? It's hard to tell. Jabbering to myself, I feel an idiot. I want to reach you. Yet I understand your silence, I think we're two of a kind. We just have different ways of keeping others at arm's length. Before I moved in to your house, I never felt too close to anyone—not even Linda.

You know, you're a funny kid. I've been watching you unwrap your Crunchie Bar. It's the gold wrapper you really wanted. You held it up to the sun, and the sweet fell on the ground and a labrador ran off with it. I offered you a bite of mine. You took it, but you didn't mind losing your Crunchie. You folded the gold wrap carefully, like a treasure map, and tucked it away in your pocket.

They have come to the park, and Steffie runs to the swings and sits there, waiting for Paul to come and push him. Paul feels sorry for him. It is like watching himself, Paul-Turner-One-Three-Six-Fraser-Street-Tauranga, snooping round graves and sitting beside the headstones while other children play in groups and gangs. But he won't push Steffie. "I think you're too big for swings," he says.

Steffie stares at other boys his age, who stand up on their bike pedals and hurtle round and round the field. He swings by himself, but soon the swing slows and Steffie slumps, head dangling, sandals scuffing. Paul goes across and nudges him.

"I guess you'd like a bicycle, like them?"

Steffie stares at Paul; in the dark iris Paul sees his reflection. "Well, would you? You'll never get anything unless you learn to ask." Steffie lowers his gaze and the leprechaun disappears.

"That won't work with me," Paul says, not softly. "If you want anything, you tell me straight. I'm not going to play guessing games with you."

Steffie doesn't move. Paul walks away. The wind is rising and he sits hunched, his back to the brick shelter wall, his arms wrapped round his chest. Steffie twists the swing ropes which tangle and untangle, spinning him. Paul waits. The boys leave on their bicycles. Steffie sidles over to Paul.

"Home, James?" They reach the dairy. The labrador is still there, sniffing round the wastepaper bin. It turns and trots after Steffie and Paul, who suddenly laughs out loud, nudging Steffie. "Hey, guess what? I used to be afraid of dogs, and now I don't think I am." He starts to jog. Steffie breaks into his jerky run, leaving behind the park and the dog, passing the flower-beds and the filter stations, rounding the corner, heading for home.

Paul gets up at six o'clock and eats breakfast by the window.

He lets himself out quietly and strides to the main road. He has to hitch-hike, for the market garden is in the Henderson Valley, off the bus route. People aren't indifferent; he usually gets a ride. He doesn't take a watch. Often he works on with the Dane for hours. There is a rhythm and a silence to the job. The cabbages are to be cut. What else is there to say? Side by side, they work the long rows. When his back aches he straightens and looks along the horizontal lines, their blue-greenness living rivulets in the dead earth. In the emptiness, sounds hang sharply—the chuck of the Dane's culling-knife chops up the hours. His footfall sucks at the mud, releasing it with a sigh.

When they break for lunch, the Dane boils a billy on his primus and they drink sweet, whisky-coloured tea from enamel mugs. While Paul eats Olga's sandwiches, his companion rolls a cigarette and smokes quietly, squatting on his haunches, his gaze assessing the harvest. A few paddocks back, cauliflowers and silverbeet are patiently maturing. The holding is small—just enough to return a modest living. Paul senses an inbuilt self-sufficiency to do, he guesses, with working hand in hand with nature. It is peaceful, tedious work. Paul sometimes shares that peace, seeing the wind shake and ripple the acmena leaves and sparrows flit along the hedge-lines.

The Dane draws his last, thrifty inhalation and stubs the butt against his boot sole. He is like that: thorough, cautious. He seems satisfied with Paul. To begin with, Paul felt he had to prove himself against the aches and weariness of physical labour. Now he feels relaxed, as though the work is teaching him there is no hurry, ripening will occur without his influence. His muscles have responded and his mind seems less anxious. He feels more a part of what he does. When the Dane has to take the cabbages to market, Paul helps him load the pallets and watches the truck bump away over the rough track. He goes back to work, reaping the hard green globes alone.

In the evenings he eats a dinner twice as large as usual. He relaxes by the fire then, not talking much, his body loose, Olga's and the children's company satisfying him.

Helen would like to show Dennis how grateful she feels.

It has been a worrying day from the moment Dinah fell and broke her arm. First there was the visit to the local doctor, then the referral to the public hospital for X-rays. There were long waits at Casualty, in the examination cubicle, outside the Plaster Room. All that time, Dennis took care of them, bringing coffee from the vending machine, coaxing Dinah through her fright and tears. Now Dinah is safely asleep, her arm propped on a pillow and her pain eased with Disprin and stories.

Helen turns to Dennis, saying softly, "Thank you very much for being there today." And she yawns, a yawn that won't be reasoned or frowned away, and Dennis tries to reorganize his hopes. He's used to that; you'd think it would be easy. Somehow it isn't. He even feels a little angry.

Helen notices his silence. "You must find me very disappointing," she says. Men presumably do, for none have stayed to make more permanent acquaintance of her. "You are disappointed, aren't you?" Preparing to say, Of course not, Dennis suddenly changes his mind. She is right, he feels let-down. It could have been good here with Helen—not necessarily the start of anything, no vast commitment, but a warm and satisfying sexual experience to remind himself he's still capable of pleasing a woman, pleasuring Helen, feeling some joy and point to living.

"Yes," he says. "I suppose I'm disappointed."

It's good to hear him say what he wants, thinks Helen—not assuming any rights, just telling her.

It's ages since she had sex. Not many opportunities since Dinah, and since Dinah she's more wary. Quietly, Helen leads Dennis to the bedroom, pulls off her jersey, unhooks her bra, lies down beside him.

Marian applies for a job as a cosmetic consultant.

She goes for an interview, where the work is explained to her. The potentials of *The Alchemoist Experience* seem almost limitless, based as they are on inter-provincial competition and maximum output incentives which, for the most productive team, include an overseas trip to the parent company in San Francisco.

Marian is dazzled when she gets the job. Her qualifications are right. She has ambition, spare time, her own car, and she is keen to learn. While she will call on people in their homes, Marian is told she must never think of herself as a door-to-door saleswoman. *The Alchemoist Experience* speaks to lonely, housebound women, changing their lives as well as their looks. It is, in a sense, a type of social work. Marian enrolls for the training programme two weeks away, and writes a cheque on her housekeeping allowance for the sample case of creams and oils. There won't be much to eat this week, but, thinks Marian, Who cares? She sits before her mirror, dreamily sniffing her transforming fluids, inhaling their sweet formulae of escape and independence.

Olga can smell jasmine.

She has carried her little carved table to a corner of the overgrown back yard, where the winter sun can penetrate, to write a letter to her sister. She settles, pen and paper ready, the sunlight behind her, but it is hard to make a start. She had forgotten the letters stuffed into her bag—found them only this morning, when Lilah wanted bus money. One was an invitation to a wedding, which Olga will happily accept, for the Patels are former neighbours and old friends of hers. But Kathleen's letter—another matter altogether. Olga opens it and reads it again.

To my dear, a question only, it has bothered me to know, and who else? In a sense coming apart, wheels pistons pieces bits. Skin-shed, speckled showers, the advertising contradictory as with dandruff or dry scalp. With your thick strong hair, how could you know? My dear, if only, if only you did, but that is how it is. Bitter hard. The happiness of those childish dreaming days, if only we could share again. But it never was, was it, dear? The cow-barn and pats, like mud-pies, warm, hardly a bad smell (well vegetarian, and chlorophyll eaters, so naturally a sweet breath). Isn't that what they say? The neighbours here are hostile and whispering, whispering. Take care. The mind is so vulnerable and must be safeguarded. I am quite well again. My own dear company an endless source of discovery and plaisir. Now then, bypassing the watchers, slip away to the post, lest at this very moment a tea break increases suspicion. We must be very careful. My dearest dreaming wishes to your loves as always. A visitation not impossible, my prayers a token, hardly more? Your Kathleen, evermore.

The sun is really hot, burning through Olga's black jumper. She scratches and wriggles like a basking cat. Not a soul to consider but herself. Steffie and Lilah at school, Paul at work, Rowan nursing. At such times she can forget the business of cooking and cleaning-up. She can sit and find a stillness where growth can take place, as in the motionless trees and plants.

But there is Kathleen to consider. Kathleen, who is evidently not well, not well at all. Squinting, for the reflection from the white page dazzles her, Olga writes, *Dear Kathleen, I had your letter yesterday...*

Olga looks expectantly around the garden. She can't say, as she is inclined to do, *and you are clearly off your rocker and, dear, into the hospital as quick as you can...*

There is a lovely little geranium peeping through the broken garden seat. Pink, with a cerise-striped heart. Without touching the ivy-like leaves, she tries to conjure that confusing, half-sweet, half-unpleasant smell. She checks. Pepper? Yes, very strange, a geranium's scent. Olga writes, *I am sitting in the garden and the geranium is in bloom.* But that isn't what she set out to say.

Last evening, how restful! Steffie and Lilah, contented with their new toys. Paul taking coffee in her boudoir, sharing the treasures she has unearthed; 78s, not a scratch on them, Haydn's *Lark Quartet* and Falla's *Three Cornered Hat,* both bought for a song, a song.

The jasmine she tied up last summer with old fishing-line needs pruning. Like a head of luxuriant hair escaping its pins, it threatens to tumble down on top of her, its branches looped, all bundled anyhow. A few starry white flowers glisten against the greenery. Another unforgettable perfume, it transports her straight to some Eastern garden where veiled women walk in pairs, whispering. The courtyard bubbles with light but the shadows look deep and secretive. *Jasmine as well,* Olga writes, *in bloom already. The winter has been mild.*

Indeed it isn't like winter at all. Olga strips off the woollen jersey and shuts her eyes. Like that, she notices sounds—a rattling car, birds' shrill squawks and chatterings, the wind in the kauri tops like breakers on a distant reef. The cats come outside. The grey sits but does not settle on the garden seat, watching the ginger, which rolls and wriggles as though it knows how its neck ruff shines in the sun. It paws the air. The grey stares down, its eyes jade-cold, its skinny tail lashing slowly.

This idea of competition amuses Olga. She has sat out on her rickety steps watching first one neighbour, then another, work hard to better what they have. Decks, railings, pergolas, pagodas have appeared, while the pink house has subsided another few inches on its footings. Oh, if she's honest with herself she'll admit there's nothing wrong with money. Say she won some heavenly fellowship, she'd have a whale of a time. Painting, plumbing, all that could be dealt with. Then . . . Her fingers trace the carvings round her table. Beneath the wooden palm trees, steps take her to an embarkation platform where she steps aboard a dhow laden with spices; clove, cinnamon, cardamon. The deck is rocking her, the bridge is curving overhead as she floats gently on, on, out to sea . . .

Disturbed by the horrible wail of the cats, Olga opens her eyes. The ginger has fled. The grey sits, contented, its back leg sticking stiffly out as it licks and licks its fur. It springs on Olga, purring, and the writing pad falls down. Olga strokes its hot, silky coat. It has a jealous nature, well, so it was born—no point in chiding it.

Olga reclaims the pad, its paper curling at the edges, and sets it on the table. The varnish smells. The heat is doing it no good, but it is old and used, bought at a jumble sale for three and sixpence when Rowan was still a toddler clinging round her mother's skirts. Your children leave; regrets will not change that, nor scolding make a whit of difference to the grey cat's nature. Olga sighs, rubs her pen tip caressingly behind his ear, and scribbles, *We are all well, children, pets, and sundries. If you need anything, if there is anything I can do, if you need a place to stay, remember you are always welcome here.*

The guard on Marian's chimney-pot is spinning, slowing, spinning. Olga sighs again. It is so peaceful in the garden; a time to be alone, to feel complete.

SEVEN

OLGA HATES HOSPITALS.

They remind her the world is a systematic and a powerful place where institutions spread silent nets, patiently awaiting their catch. A slip, a trip, are all it takes to qualify.

"And how's the hospital?" Olga tries to sound enthusiastic. Beyond sense and reason it may be to her to work in such a place, but it is her daughter's choice.

"Fine," says Rowan cheerfully. "Kathleen came in, but she doesn't seem to recognise me. I'm nursing her."

"Poor Kathleen." Olga speaks with feeling. She has been in hospital three times to have her babies. Childbirth was painful, yet it had a certain power. The intrusion came later—certainly of her body, with staff examining her breasts and private places; and, more devastatingly, of her independence. I won't be ordered, thought Olga. But she was. The hospital saw to it. There were rules and Olga had to bow. Rules for feeding, ways of bathing, times for nurturing the babies. Rules for patients, and visitors, for tucking in the sheets, for putting out the lights. Other women lay back, luxuriating, saying what a wonderful rest it was. Olga, tethered to her bed by stitches and post-partum bleeding, fumed like a furious cat shut up in a carton, preparing its spring for freedom.

"She'll get better. Don't worry." Rowan means to be reassuring and Olga feels guilty. While Kathleen has to be held in seclusion and dosed with powerful sedatives, Olga will not have to visit her.

"Will you and Paul sign this?" Rowan pulls a crumpled paper from her pocket. "It's a petition from the hospital. We want to stop the council cutting down the old magnolia trees in the front garden. They want the land for motorway extensions."

"I'll sign, of course!" Olga scribbles with a flourish, glad to forget about Kathleen. "I'm sure Paul will. I'll ask him tonight. Just leave this on the mantelpiece."

"It's getting late." Rowan sighs as she secures the petition with the French clock. "I'll miss the bus if I don't go."

"Stay overnight, darling." Olga brushes back a wisp of Rowan's hair, the way she used to when Rowan came home dishevelled after school. Rowan smiles at her.

"I can't. I'm on duty early, and tonight I have to study."

"They work you far too hard," grumbles Olga. Rowan kisses her.

"I'm all right. Don't forget, ask Paul to sign. We might have to demonstrate as well."

"Count us in!" says Olga, happy there's one aspect of the hospital she can identify with. "One thing we have in common, Paul and I love trees."

Kathleen's my aunt," Rowan tells Josie.

"I used to stay with her when I was small. She had a cottage at the beach. I was washed off the rocks there, once. I nearly drowned. She fed me pancakes. I think that's all she could cook. Pancakes, every day. She was strange; kind, though. She never bossed me around or made a fuss. She used to talk to herself. She'd walk up and down, pushing the hand-mower, chatting away. Children don't worry about that sort of thing, do they? They take it for granted. I did. She let me do what I liked—eat or not, go to bed or stay up. Sometimes we went looking for *pipis*. There were pinholes in the smooth sand, and frothy bubbles where the shellfish hid. I helped carry seaweed for her garden. Ugh, slimy, revolting."

"Mmmm," Josie murmurs. She is lying on her bed, reading a paperback. The cover displays a naked woman over whom a huge man wields a bull-whip. Josie reads fast, flicking the pages over, chewing toffees.

"I do think it's strange, Josie. She used to look after me, and now here she is in my ward and I'm taking care of her—as though I know how to make her better. And I don't."

"You don't have to. That's the doctors' job! Does Jacob know she's your relative?"

"Yes," says Rowan shortly. When she asked to be assigned care of her aunt, Jacob looked doubtful and warned her against personal involvement. "You'd think caring was dangerous. By the way, Olga signed the petition, and she's asking Paul."

"Good." Josie chews, skimming pages. "He's making her do it by the zodiac. She's had eleven orgasms, there's only Pisces now. Do you have orgasms?"

"I'm a virgin." Rowan sounds ashamed.

"So what? I'm frigid. That's what Terry says."

"I wouldn't believe anything he says."

"Don't you like him?"

"I think he's awful to you. And if you were frigid, you wouldn't want to sleep with him."

"I guess." Resigned, Josie takes a sweet.

"We said we'd study tonight," Rowan reminds her.

"Help yourself," says Josie. Rowan takes a Harrogate toffee.

Do you know who I am, Kathleen? I'm Rowan. I've come to help you dress.

"It's cold, Kathleen, and you have no clothes on. Your hand's cold. Feel this, it's made of wool. Put it on and you'll be warm.

"You seem frightened. I won't hurt you, I'm Rowan. I work here at the hospital. I've come to help you dress.

"Here's your singlet and pants. Why are you laughing? There, that's good, now the other leg, and the arm through here.

"You can't do up the buttons? Here, let me. Tuck yourself in. Now the blue cardigan. Aren't you warmer?

"Your hair's full of knots. Here's the comb. Don't tear your hair like that, don't cry.

"You're safe. Nothing will happen. The people here are kind. Hold my hand, Kathleen. Yours is so cold. Don't cry."

I'm a doctor, Kathleen.

"Now, the question is, Why haven't you been taking your medication?

"According to this letter, you were throwing rocks on your neighbours' roof and shouting abuse at them? You said they were out to get you, and you had means of stopping them? Now all this can be kept in check if you take your Melleril. You know that.

"Nurse, this young man with me is a psychology graduate who is observing my patients. Observe the mannerisms, John? Obviously hallucinating. By the way, this rash is a side-effect of major tranquillisers. We'll chat about the long-term effects later . . . tachycardia, jaundice, eye damage, extrapyramidal and metabolic reactions, various other problems.

"Well Kathleen, we're not getting very far with you today, are we? Nurse, your patient will have her hair out by the roots if you don't restrain her.

"We'll push on, John. Have a browse through her case history, it's quite interesting.

"See you tomorrow, Kathleen. Now you cooperate with nurse. Remember, we only want to help you get better quickly."

You know me now, Kathleen. I'm Rowan, your niece.

"Let's walk out in the garden today? The daffodils are out, and the camellias.

"What's your garden like now? You kept it so nicely when I used to come and stay. There's lots of birds where I live, and bush. The houses seem to have just grown there like trees do.

"The doctor wants you to go to Group soon. People talk about their problems and there's a leader who keeps the group together. It's good you're well enough to go. You are much better. You know that, don't you?

"It's cold, let's keep walking. I'll show you the magnolia trees in the front garden. The council want to cut them down. People are funny, aren't they, Kathleen?"

As your group leader, I want you all to meet our new member, Kathleen.

"We meet at two o'clock every afternoon, Kathleen. Sometimes there's just a few, sometimes a dozen or more. We come together to share. We want you to feel welcome and participate.

"Do you want to say anything? No? Then we'll introduce ourselves. I'm Trudy, and going round the circle, Michael, speak up, Michael. . .

"Please don't cry, Kathleen. We're your friends, we only want to help you."

"How's Kathleen?" asks Olga, when Rowan next comes home.

"Much better."

"How much better?" Olga seeks reprieve; a week, a day.

"Ready for visitors," says cheerful Rowan.

Olga sighs and says, "Well, that's good news."

Paul has changed, thinks Rowan.

She looks at him as he sits by the fire, his long legs stretched out, his eyes half closed. He's not taller, or fatter; his curly hair is just the same. Perhaps it's the woollen shirt that makes him look more solid. He's relaxed—tired, probably. Outdoor work is tiring. So is nursing.

She examines her legs in the firelight. They've grown bigger, she decides. She wishes she was elegant, a model with groomed hair and an air of *ennui*. Jacob might notice her then. For months she's loved a man who does not see her as a woman. He's been polite and kind, assigned her duties, taught her dosages, discussed the patients in her care. Standing beside him in the tiny medication room, she's felt his presence strongly, subtly. The drugs her patients take must work like that—secretly slipping through the bloodstream, carrying imperatives of surrender. She has wanted to be swept away in Jacob, to abandon career, family, principles, herself. And he's unaware of her.

She wishes he was elsewhere, far away. It's all very well for Josie, laughing at her, saying Jacob's a father figure, and Rowan an idiot. All that is very well.

Rowan wakes slowly.

That's how it used to be before the time of clattering clocks and mad dashes through the rain to the nurses' station.

It must be late. Sunlight probes the splits in the curtains.

Lilah has slipped off like a snake, shedding the wrinkled skin of her unmade bed. The ginger cat is heavily curled on Rowan's feet. She pokes it with her toe. It pretends to be asleep.

Rowan shifts and stretches. Saturdays were the best, she thinks.

A tide of Saturdays rushes over her, tumbling head over heels in the exhilaration of childhood when you were making memories, not re-living them. Everything was fresh, Home was real life. Where is Jacob among the household jabs of argument, the surges of sudden laughter? Her yearning falls away. Jacob is a dream. I don't need him, Rowan experiments.

No disaster follows. She can hear the peach branch, tapping, tapping at the window. She jumps out of bed and dashes in her pyjamas to the kitchen where Olga stands, cutting onions at the bench. She throws her arms around Olga and squeezes so hard that Olga laughs, helpless, the knife in her hand, tears from the onion juice running down her cheeks.

Olga hardly raises an objection about the soccer match.

How can she, seeing Steffie hop and Rowan scuffle in the drawer for her school scarf?

For Rowan it's a trip back to childhood, to winter mornings when she ironed her blouse and whitened her sandshoes and caught the bus to the netball courts and home again, late in the day, her cheeks glowing and a taste of hot-dogs from the tuckshop lingering.

"A hermit lived there." Rowan points out the house to Paul. "We'd follow her, out walking. She'd shake a walking-stick if we went too close. She always wore a purple coat and grey beret pulled down to her ears. Her legs were straight up and down in wrinkled stockings, like an old lady in a picture book. We'd call out names as we ran past her house and she'd come to the gate and throw stones after us. I helped with the *Save the Children* collection for a few years. We went to the door and she pulled a roll of money out of her bloomer elastic and gave it to us. There was over a hundred dollars. The next year she just stared through the window and shook her stick. A while after that she died. No one knew for a week."

"It's that kind of district," Paul replies. "The first thing I noticed was its secret nature—as though the gardens were watching, saying, Who's this stranger? The house numbers were like a treasure hunt. The bush was so still, yet alive. And when I turned the corner and came to your place, it was like a dream . . . I'd dreamed of a tower, and there it was."

"I didn't want you to come," Rowan says, "I was sick of boarders."

"I'm forgiven?"

"Yes."

"I'm not the boarder now?"

"Just Paul."

Paul smiles and so does Rowan. Steffie zigzags ahead.

They go faster to catch up with him.

Steffie is uncertain at the soccer field.

He stays near Paul and Rowan, staring as parents on the sidelines shout, Don't hang about, get in there! Lovely build-up! Oh, good ball! He stares at the women in trousers and parkas, who wave and yell and groan when a boy sprawls face-down in the mud. He stares at the players. He stares at the umpire. Once, a kick spirals the ball towards him and instinctively he lifts his hands. He makes the catch and stares as though the moon has landed in his arms.

"You can have a ball if you like," says Paul. "You only have to ask." Steffie tugs Paul's hand and takes him over to the changing sheds. He touches the shining spokes of the bicycle chained there, and hops and hops.

Olga," says Paul, "Steffie wants a bike."

Olga feels her face grow pinched and disapproving.

Paul is talking on, saying how Steffie's co-ordination would improve and his sense of pride develop. And Rowan backs him up, while Steffie hops from one foot to the other. Their triple face, bright and alive from the outing in the frosty air, pins her like a searchlight.

"We could never afford such a thing," she says without hope.

"Why not start a fund? Steffie's bike fund. If we set aside a little each week it will soon grow."

"Well . . ." Olga senses reprieve. She has never found that money grows.

"No broken-down old wreck," adds Paul. "New and shiny—you'd like that, wouldn't you?"

"Then I want skates," says Lilah, loudly, and Steffie hops and hops.

Olga asks Paul to help clear out the basement bedroom.

"My sister will be coming to stay—unless you'd like a change yourself?"

Paul certainly would not. In his tower, the ladder cover closed, he's above the household, above the world, as empty as a lazy lizard on a rock. He drags Olga's hoard into the yard and surveys it critically. Olga wants it, every single thing.

"I must keep the auger, and the pit-saw, they are virtually antique. And that treadle fretsaw is a museum piece if I can find the missing bits. They're here somewhere."

"I suppose you want to keep this rusty fence wire and this torn fishing net?"

"I will mend it. Meanwhile roll it up and put it in the rain barrel. Now that funny little clothesline is invaluable. See how the pole fits in, like this, and it holds the smalls for the entire family."

"All this is only fit for the next inorganic rubbish collection, Olga."

"My genealogy charts! Look at them, how mouldy they are, this dreadful climate! Pass me out the spinning-wheel, Paul—the spindle's broken but a screw or two will put that right. And there is the mower blade! What a day of treasures this is turning out to be!"

I'd like to ask Kathleen if there's anything to share with us today. Kathleen? The Group would love to hear about you. Nothing? Not today? Never mind, don't worry. There's all the time in the world. Perhaps Angela will tell us how she did with the list we thought up yesterday. Did you set the tables? Pick flowers? Help at suppertime? I'm disappointed, Angela. You did agree to try. Derek, did you write off for that job? Sit down, please, Derek, and stop changing the subject—Kathleen isn't interested in your scars. Michael, I can't understand you. The Group would rather hear a simple statement. What did you have for breakfast? Scramble? Eggs? That's very good. And Rita, how's the diet? We all feel, Kathleen, that Rita's looking much more attractive since she decided to lose weight. You went to MacDonalds, Rita? Well, that's a shame. Are you going to tell us all exactly what you ate? The Group would like to hear. I wonder how we all feel, knowing Rita has broken her promise to us? Kathleen dear, there's no need to cry, we're all friends here, we care for one another."

Jacob looks at Rowan.

He notices a change in her as she confronts him across the desk.

"Kathleen refuses to go to Group. She's withdrawn. I don't think her treatment is effective."

"I see," says Jacob pleasantly. "And now you are the doctor?"

"I am her nurse."

"That's right. That's what you are."

"She keeps telling me she wants her voices back. She talks of death. She doesn't want her medication."

"You think that is a good idea? She is your aunt, there is bound to be over-identification."

"I don't understand," Rowan argues, "it's as though she has no rights."

"True enough—she gave up many of those on admission. Do you like to see the states our patients arrive in? If you do, perhaps you are in the wrong job?"

Rowan feels like crying. Jacob's words assault her and her new freedom has no substance at all.

"I will look into the problems you have raised." Jacob nods, dismissing her.

Olga arrives with daffodils.

Like a charm she carries them, exorcising authority.

The Charge Nurse is, to her surprise, a man; and one who takes her into the office and explains Kathleen's progress, intelligently, as though he knows Olga is no fool. Encouraged, Olga adds, "And Rowan? My daughter's working in this ward." Jacob nods. "A good nurse in the making. At present, a trifle intense. But who can say, perhaps better that way than the other?" And he and Olga laugh at the friction of maturity, the way it wears one back to basics.

I've brought you flowers, Kathleen."

And Olga looks round for a vase. She feels uncomfortable. Madness should be dramatized, she thinks. Shakespeare had the art of it. He knew how to make it the symbol it should be of desperate ambitions and failures. Here it is too ordinary. The people she sees look merely apathetic and untidy.

"What have you been doing?" she enquires, resisting an urge to sit up straight and keep her eye on the clock. "They say you're much better, dear."

But Olga cannot see it. Kathleen yawns and rubs her skin. Her smile is vacant, as though too much effort goes into life for her liking. Her eyes bridge the gulf, meeting her sister's. She seems to say, Here I am, Olga. Find the end of me, unravel me like knitting and wind me up and knit me differently, for I'm not much fit or use the way I am.

"You're really on the mend," says Olga quickly. "The doctors say so. So as soon as you are better you must come and stay with us. You will meet Paul. He's helped me clear the basement room for you. I've made it nice, and we shall talk and find, oh, heaps of things to do."

Olga likes to imagine that. Her mind flies from the present, a hawk on the wing above dreary tussock country.

EIGHT

"PINK IS LOVE'S COLOUR," says Olga.

She considers the table linen at Manuel's. "Salmon pink is motherlove, and the shell pink of those carnations is tolerance."

Paul smiles. She sounds so certain. "And the chairs?"

Olga surveys the velvet upholstery. "Old rose—the shade of sex."

"Then all in all the decor is well chosen."

"Indeed it is." And Olga laughs. It is her birthday. Though she pesters him, Paul won't say how he knows. A week in advance he had the copy of *Antipodean Notes 1888* searched out and wrapped, the taxi ordered, the restaurant booked. "Out with the nobs?" Olga enquired, sounding doubtful. But Paul knew how to persuade the Countess from her reticence. He eyes her now. In the gentle candlelight he sees the deep lines on her brow as underscoring a beauty changed but not destroyed by life. Her hair is in an elegant coil. Julia's aquamarine necklace sparkles as she gazes around, her manner that of a person delighted by small events. The chianti bottles, the gilt mirrors, the coats of arms and halberds all seem to please her enormously. "Such swank! As a rule my birthdays are quite unmemorable. But this treat, and the marvellous book . . . My other men could never have begun to know me as you seem to."

"Weren't you in love when you got married?"

"I've really no idea. It was so long ago."

"But wouldn't you remember?" Her detachment puzzles him. He thinks of marriage as a commitment. None of his close family is divorced. Death has been the only power to sever wife from husband.

"No," says Olga, firmly. "Men have drifted in and out of my life, but as to why we met . . . There was my husband, we married and had children, something must have made us do it, yet we had nothing in common. And then Angelo . . . Did I ever tell you how I found him in the rain and offered him a bed? He stayed for years, then off he went. Looking back, I can't see I had much choice."

Paul can't understand her cavalier attitude. She has tried on this partner or that one in the ways he must rummage through old clothing bins, hoping for a bargain, a style that suits.

"It wasn't love then," he decides for her. "Not that I would know. I've had feelings for girls and felt empty and lonely when things didn't work out, but is that love?"

"What a classifier you are! There are as many loves as lovers."

"Maybe," Paul says shortly. Love—the subject is starting to raise unpleasant associations of weakness and lack of control. I think it would take someone very clever to make me fall in love. The waiter's coming. Are you ready to order?"

He smiles as she orders *Coquille Saint Jacques à la Parisienne* and *Profiteroles au Chocolat* like a veteran gourmet.

"Yes," she continues, after Paul has given his own order and asked for wine, "love leads people a merry dance. I knew a dressmaker, in fact a highly cultured woman, who'd finally run off and left a husband who didn't care a fig for her. She'd been stranded half her life in the New Hebrides, all parties and entertaining, a dreadful provincial atmosphere. She was brought to sewing seams to eke out a living. We used to have French conversations—she would correct my accent, and I would ask her to eat with us. She was poor as a churchmouse, but terribly proud. It all became too much, and in the end she drowned herself. Tragic."

"Yes." Paul wonders why Olga's friends sound so unfortunate.

"But don't you wish you'd travelled a bit? You seem to prefer foreigners to your own people."

Olga waves her hand, dismissing his suggestion, but he persists.

"You'd adore Europe."

"Well yes. The architecture, art galleries . . . Still, I'll never have the money and that's that."

"We can travel in our heads, at least." And as the food is served and the wine poured they plan their world tour, Paul liking the route through Asia and India, Olga heading northeast to the Pacific and Africa. "We are such an isolated dot on the map, there are infinite possibilities of escape. I might go, one day," says Paul.

"Another Durrell, or Van der Post," sighs Olga. "I don't mean to pry, but how is your writing? I notice when you slip off to your room, you know. I can always guess you're in the throes of creativity."

Paul doesn't want to disappoint her. Privacy is important to him and so are secrets, even dull ones like lying on his mattress, eating biscuits, dreaming. His creative spirit, fanned by Olga, has uses she doesn't suspect. It is an excellent excuse for getting out of the dishes. "Nothing is quite finished," he says, feeling guilty as Olga searches for some way to help. She leans forward, releasing the perfume she has dabbed on from the *Lalique* scent-bottle, the one for special occasions. "You must simply dive in, Paul. You think too hard and undermine yourself. Now I saw a story title on the lavatory wall as I went by on the bus just yesterday. *Hawks and Doves.* Isn't it perfect? And my mind had created a plot in a trice. Naturally I placed it in the Crusade period. A young knight, Gawain, a boy of noble birth, is the dove. He is already schooled in the arts of manners, singing, playing, languages. He must go to his uncle for instruction in battle skills. The uncle, of course, is the hawk. He covets Gawain's lady-love. Well, there was a story half-made in a minute, less. History's riddled with plots. There's nothing new on the face of the earth. Take any example—the road toll. Riding accidents were very common. My great-aunt's cousin was thrown out of a pony trap and broke her neck. You could write about that."

"Thank you, Olga, but you'd better keep your plots. You've far more imagination than I have."

"You're very kind," Olga agrees, "but I've had too much wine, never mind imagination. I know you can write, Paul. But what exactly do you want to write *about?*"

"The truth; that's the trouble." He expects her to laugh.

"I know it's elusive," she sympathizes, "I come across the problem all the time, reading history. Different perspectives and different versions. They'd have you believe everyone used to die of murder or the plague or gangrene, but it's rubbish. The Crusaders used herbal remedies—and that I came across quite by accident. People only started to die off like flies from the sixteenth century, when doctors discovered chemicals. Now that I *could* write about."

Paul is quiet. He feels alone, enclosed in a puzzle he can't share with anyone, for it is private. Olga may unroll the fascinating tapestries of the past before his eyes and he is tempted. For Olga, they may reflect her truth as she defines herself against the characteristics of ages, centuries. It has not helped Paul to look outside in space or time. His search is different. He can't pinpoint it; he is closer to it, that's all he can say, when he is alone, cross-legged on his mattress, emptied of desires and thoughts; or absorbed in the physical labours of the market garden. Losing his sense of self, he feels closer to an inner centre. It is a paradox, not one he can explain to himself, much less to Olga.

She reaches across the table and rests her hand on his. He looks down, noticing his work-worn skin, and the small cracks along her index finger. "How little your hand is." He feels surprised. She seems so resilient, he is startled by the fragile feel of her.

"People weren't always well-fed and fat. Small and wiry, they were. Richard the Lionheart's armour would have fitted me."

Paul imagines Olga full-tilt in battle, and he laughs so that people look at them. Olga does not seem displeased. She extends an imperious arm. "Assist me, Sir Gawain." Paul watches her make a *prima donna's* exit and follows after her. "I love you, Olga—you are such a show-off." She smiles at him, quoting, "And you, Paul, my very perfect gentle knight."

"Your carriage," says Paul, handing Olga in to the back seat and following. The taxi sweeps them along the spinning nightlights and alleys of an unfamiliar route.

"Relax, Paul," Olga murmurs, "there's more than one way home." Paul leans back and shuts his eyes. It's a tempting sensation, adrift of any reference point. Like that, it seems natural to accept the willing clasp of Olga's hand, her yielding press against him.

Marian wishes she had friends.

Until the point was made at the *Alchemoist* workshop that friends are one of the better sales resources, she had done quite well without them. Now she perches on the breakfast stool, a district map and her brand-new appointment diary open on the divider, staring through the window. Olga is in the yard, apparently dozing in the fitful sunshine. Callers often trail up Olga's overgrown path. Over the years Marian has watched the procession—every age, race, and colour, she has sometimes thought. What do they come for? Olga has nothing to sell.

Marian knows every human transaction has a point. Dennis doesn't like that kind of talk. He would call her calculating when she is only being realistic. He would be shocked if Marian said, as she often feels inclined to, You have always used financial control to make me dependent; do you blame me if I have paid you back in the coin women use?

Dennis would reply, Why Marian, I've always given you what you wanted, as far as I was able. He would sound sincere and he would look hurt, hurt again by hurtful Marian. Well, she will no longer set out to hurt and deny Dennis. Fighting takes energy. Now she would rather have power; the power of money and self-determination. Oh, some people would call her materialistic and unfeeling. She knows these aren't the goals parents instil into their children. She went to Bible class, she learned the Christian values, love and giving. Somehow they rubbed away as easily as sunburn. She never could believe such values led to happiness. Certainly she hasn't been happy living with Dennis. She can see what dependence has done to her. How moody you become, and how nasty . . . She can't wait to get out from under his thumb.

With her brightly polished fingernail she traces the district's web of streets and cul-de-sacs. Trapped; yes, that's how it feels to sit at home as she has, waiting. Now it's time to start. *The Alchemoist Experience* doesn't sell itself, though. It operates through strategy. Marian has the techniques. Since the training course she feels equipped with power. Her gilded tools are ready. She can't wait to give an *Alchemoist* party with its games and prizes. She only needs the friends, to demonstrate the magic a changed self-image can achieve.

Olga's still there, staring at the trees. She'll never change, she'll be there at seventy in her decrepit garden, going nowhere. Poor thing, thinks Marian. Her life must be so dull. Surely a party would liven things for Olga, and for Marian? Why, they've been neighbours for years. That must count as friendship?

Taking her cosmetic display case and her diary, Marian goes to visit Olga.

Olga would be delighted.

Yes, happy, to arrange a little party on Marian's account. She's used to odd requests—and Marian has implied that Olga, as hostess, will herself receive certain discounts and rewards. Olga inspects Marian's goods. She wants them. While good old lanoline does, the display of such items on Julia's dressing-table would be fitting, somehow. Certainly Olga will rustle up a few friends for Marian.

Olga sits on in the garden.

She should be busy. The basement room must be cleared for Kathleen and a present found for the Patels' wedding. Ah well, thinks Olga, it can wait. Most things can, most urgency is self-invented. She feels weak and light-headed. She's noticed the symptoms several times recently. Hardly to be wondered at today, she's not used to rich food and drink. A chill makes her shiver. The wind is gusty even in this sheltered corner where any sun finds its way as though to a burning-glass. Marian's chimney-cover twirls round and round like a merry-go-round. The trees creak and rock. A bird careers from its high kauri perch, eddying as though it's drunk or mad. No, such fates are not for birds—they have simpler lives.

She can't help thinking the human lot lacks something. Take Kathleen, better now, they say. There she sits in the hospital, dazed-looking, as someone might sit outside a home razed by a demolition squad. Her small-talk tries to agree, Yes, I must rebuild; the trouble is, what materials am I to use, who am I to ask for help? She says she's tired. Olga had to stare sharply at her, wondering if she'd really heard her sister ask, Is sleep like death?

Of course Kathleen must come and stay. Olga has never turned away a stranger, she can't refuse her sister. Yet everything is peaceful and steady as it is. And that is the way she likes it.

Sometimes she feels she's known it all—poverty, frustration, violence, drunkenness. They have sunk to the bed of her life stream and over all of them she has tumbled, taking the bruises, putting up with the pain. The present feels like a deep and sheltered pool. She wants to keep it that way. It's true, Paul hurt her last night, suddenly drawing back, rejecting her, saying, No, Olga, nothing like that, it wouldn't work: and climbing up to his tower and slamming down the ladder cover as though doubting her intentions; or his own, for there was no mistaking those mutual currents, the oldest lure between a man and woman. She put on Julia's nightgown and went to bed alone, her knees drawn close, cocooned against the loneliness, thinking to herself, the devil take tomorrow and cold Paul.

But perhaps he was right in wanting to keep the *status quo*. Impulse was always her downfall. Warnings from her mother never did a whit of good. She has never cared about the future. It has taken Paul to help her understand another perspective. He does not make false promises. Being made like him must leave one always worrying—whatever you did would imply conflict. It's just as well she has Paul to lean on now. Living like that would make her tired.

Rowan faces Jacob.

"I've seen the ward changes," she says. "I'll miss this ward awfully."

Jacob observes her. Her skirt is creased, and one stocking laddered. Her fair hair straggles like a child's.

"We must move on," he says. "Your experience will broaden." Some of the patients take advantage of her, he feels. He's aware some manipulate as cunningly as any other person under pressure.

"There's something else," says Rowan, blushing, and she thrusts a sheet of paper over the desk.

"What is this about?" He sounds brusque, feeling some claim pressed on him. Sometimes his wife confronts him that way, explaining nothing, her whole posture a stance of expectation. He longs to escape from emotional demands. He sees enough of those.

"The nurses are signing a petition to save the old magnolia trees. The motorway extensions cut through the garden."

Jacob feels the gulf of age between them. To believe signatures on a page will halt a sacrifice whose hour has come . . . But then, she's young, almost a child herself. To get rid of her, he scribbles down his name and Rowan beams.

"Thank you very much. We intend to protest too."

"Good luck to you," says Jacob. If he sounds paternal, it can't be helped. That is what she draws from him.

I'm not really interested in philosophy," Helen says. "I wish I'd enrolled for psychology instead."

She streches a slim leg, admiring the new nail polish. It's been years since she bothered to make up, paint her nails. There's no point when you live alone. But Dennis likes her to take trouble. They've been spending more time together. Perhaps that's why her interest in

Aristotle and Bentham has dwindled. "Maybe I should drop out."

"I don't think so. You'll have something to show for the year if you stick out the last term."

Helen sighs and sits up, the flesh of her belly making a small fold which Dennis runs his tongue along.

"I could finish my term essay in a day if Dinah wasn't so demanding. It's her broken arm."

"I'll mind her."

"How could you?"

"I've a leave day due."

"You wouldn't waste it with Dinah?"

"I don't think it would be a waste," Dennis says.

Paul and Steffie walk single-file.

The bush paths feel sleek and wet. It is a secret world, this kaleidoscope of flickers, rustles, wing-beats, rushings where the rains run down and fill the streambeds. Steffie stands before the muscled trunk of the huge kauri. Gum glistens like tears. He twists off a chunk and tastes its resin-scent.

They slither downhill, grabbing brush and branches to slow their passage. There are hardly any animals; none of the impressive beasts that live in picture-book forests. They've only ever found small, humble-looking creatures; bush-rats, hedgehogs, sometimes an opossum, its bead-eyed baby clinging as it sidles by at dusk. Steffie's not much interested in animals. He can by-pass motionless creatures with hardly a glance. Birds flying make him stand and stare. It's not their form but their motion that holds him, Paul thinks. Their worlds seem split and at the same time complementary, as though Paul sees the objects there and Steffie the spaces in between.

The stream's rushing is louder. The deeper bush smells smoky, feels chilly. Two wood-pigeons break cover and dive, floating on the valley, near enough for Paul to see the irridescent purple and green of their chest feathers. They gather themselves and together climb up and up, and the rushing of their wings enters Paul like a spell. Steffie has run ahead to the stream. Sandals off, he squats on a stone and peers into the pools' shadows, smiling secretly.

You are an eel, thinks Paul—slippery, acquainted with silence, deep water. You don't want to take my bait and let me draw you up into the light. But I'm patient; I can wait.

Paul shows Steffie the weta skin he's found.

Brittle, it has the texture and colour of burnt toffee. Hooks line its legs. The outer form stays perfect. "A creature lived in here. This was its old coat. It left it behind and made a new one. Maybe it was tired of being locked inside. I think I'm like that, are you?" Steffie takes the shell and crumples it to powder and runs away from Paul.

In any case Paul doesn't care. He's not much inclined to teach Steffie today. He's tired, uneasy. There's something inhabiting him, restless as a hatching chick; some feeling to do with the pink house and the tower and Olga.

Last night he could have done what he felt like, thrown caution to the winds and gone to Olga. Even then the chick was stirring, warning against . . . But he's not sure, it will not hatch, he only knows it's safer to keep to himself and guard his independence.

Dennis arranges his leave day.

Dinah doesn't object when Helen leaves. She seems pleased to have Dennis to herself. She bounces wildly on the sofa. "Look at *me*."

Dennis sits patiently. How is it, he wonders, that with this child he works from some wise centre, able to focus on her needs instead of her behaviour? Children are such a clear lens. Happiness and pain focus so sharply through their eyes. He's used to offering help to needy clients but Dinah reaches deeper into him, as though he's recently found buried needs within himself.

Dinah presses crayons and paper on Dennis. "Draw me a horse."

"I'll try. I'm not much good."

She giggles. "That's not a horse."

"I warned you."

"Let me." She demonstrates. "And that's you."

It's not a bad caricature, he thinks. He points out the legs, which lack feet. "How can I walk?"

"You can't." She sounds triumphant. "So you have to stay here."

"Where did you live before, Dinah?"

"On the boat from England."

"Did you like it on the boat?"

"The rooms had signs. They said, Children are silly, they can't come in here."

"I'm sure they didn't."

"Did. Silly silly silly." She pokes out her tongue, runs away, returns with a stuffed koala bear. "This is from Australia. Mummy bought it."

"He's fine."

"No. He's too big, he can't go to bed with me."

She goes off to the kitchenette. Dennis hears clatters. She carries in a plate of animal biscuits and goes back for the glasses of orange drink, walking as though the carpet is mined. "It's a bit spilled."

"I don't mind."

Dennis has a yellow-iced lion. Dinah has a bear.

"Are we going out?"

"If you like," says Dennis.

They stroll through the village. Outside the public library there are lawns and gardens. They sit in the weak sun, eating pastries from the delicatessen. The pigeons clatter down and, making gentle, fussy noises, grab the bits of pastry Dinah throws. Sparrows dodge in for their share like children in a crowd.

"You eat some, Dinah—pastry's bad for their teeth."

"Birds don't have *teeth*."

"Of course they must, for crunching bones."

"Birds don't eat *bones*." She laughs at him. How clear her eyes are, he thinks; as though she's never been tired, never cried.

"Oh," he says, "don't they?"

Mothers come and go with small children bundled into prams or pushchairs. They leave them parked like bicycles and run into the library with their returns. The children peer out at the pigeons and at Dennis. "Today you're my daddy." And Dinah hops off the seat and takes his hand.

"If you like."

They walk slowly back to the flat.

"Now we're home," Dinah says. And Dennis feels he is.

"Can I have a drink of milk?"

As Dennis fetches it, he picks up a discarded page, part of Helen's essay, lying by the dish-drainer. *Whereas happiness as seen by Bentham was equated with pleasure, Aristotle believed it was the* result *of right action developed by habit.* Dennis reads and he smiles. The way *result* is underlined, she must have been writing from conviction, not the texts. He turns to Dinah and sees she has already fallen asleep on the sofa, her arm in the grubby plaster hanging down.

"She decided I was her daddy today," Dennis tells Helen when she comes home.

Helen doesn't laugh, as Dennis feared she might—just blushes, turns to make the coffee. He touches her arm, delaying her.

"Helen," says Dennis. "There's some decisions to be made. It's time we faced them, don't you think?"

Kathleen is sane again.

Surrounded by Olga's cheerful disorder she feels in transit, a traveller at an unscheduled port, demands in foreign babble thrust on her. It's very kind of Olga to offer hospitality. After the collective life she's been through recently, the basement room is a retreat. She doesn't mind its dark, damp atmosphere. Like a day-shy bush creature she shelters there, hearing overhead the sounds of the children, animals, visitors, Olga and the boarder. She would avoid them all, except that avoiding is impolite and touched with melancholia. It's up to her to make an effort, so she goes upstairs to sit and discover her fingers twisting, twisting. The cats, barbarians that happily torture and dismember helpless mice and lizards, spring on her and purr.

Olga's busy at the bench, chopping, slicing, throwing things in pans. Busy Olga puts to shame her sister Kathleen, sitting like that without a whit of purpose or accomplishment. They've gone such different roads, as though they never did share a bedroom, whisper, plot, cry together when the favourite working dog was going blind and father took her out and shot her by the barn.

"Father was hard," murmurs Kathleen.

Olga has noticed how her sister, who says so little, has this way of raising topics better left. She lifts the saucepan lid and stares into the bubbling water. "Lilah," Olga calls, "run out please and pick some sprigs of mint."

"But mother was the boss," adds Kathleen softly.

"Never!" Olga is offended at this outright contradiction to her own beliefs.

"She was, Olga. Cunning, too, at getting her own way."

"That's a dreadful thing to say! Father made her suffer. He was a bully, and domineering. He shot Christy when he knew the vet could save her sight. He was too mean to pay for the operation."

"Mother made him. I heard what she said. Father cried when he buried her. She was his favourite."

"He had no favourites." It is provoking, this exhuming of the past—first Rowan, now Kathleen expecting Olga to turn the whole foundation of her past topsy-turvy. The past is history.

"You were," Kathleen says, so quietly Olga has to strain her ears to hear at all.

"Rubbish!" And Olga throws the mint into the pot, and showers in the salt, and bangs the lid on, hard.

As Olga stands, the steam fuming round her face, Kathleen watches her. She's always watched. She understands their differences. Kathleen always knew thoughts were for hiding away like sixpences beneath the drawer-lining; bright coins to take out secretly and fondle. Olga never did know how to hide herself. She came right out and said what she thought and did what she liked. She didn't care how angry she made people. Kathleen sees how that small, defiant Olga's not changed a bit. She's just as she was; rat-tail plait askew, stubborn eyes aglow and begging for the tinder of opposition to make her flare and burn.

"Of course you did fight a lot with father," Kathleen agrees humbly. "I think you saw how mother hated him, I think you wanted to bear his anger for him. You were sorry for him."

Sorry for father?

Olga pokes a carving-fork into the potatoes, snatches up the pot, and pours a flood of steaming water down the sink.

Sorry for father! She dumps down the saucepan and thumps the masher up and down, and clears it on the side, bang bang bang.

Olga hurls potatoes on the dinner plates.

Sorry for him? Analysing, analysing—Kathleen must be mad.

"Anyone who wants dinner can come and get it," Olga informs the air. She collects her own plate and goes to her boudoir to eat. There, at least, she can create some semblance of sanity.

NINE

OLGA ENCOUNTERS A DOWNPOUR on her way to the Patels' wedding.

The tissue paper round her present falls apart and Julia's French clock shows through for all the guests to see. Olga's not displeased. It's a lavish gift; one Paul has disagreed with her over, saying she should give something practical and keep the heirlooms for her own family. But she doesn't feel, as he apparently does, that each friendship warrants a certain due, no more. True, the Patels moved out of her life many years ago, and even at the time they were friends more of convenience than common interest. With her husband gone, and not two ha'pence to rub together, Olga was both lonely and in need—as were the Patel family. Perhaps their exchanges of babysitting, firewood, second-hand winter clothing were mundane. Yet Olga remembered Asha's visits, her samples of Indian sweetmeats, her obvious pleasure in the heirlooms Olga brought out to show her. She had particularly admired the marble mantel clock, and that is why Olga has decided to give it to Asha's daughter, Hanu. A timepiece seems appropriate. The families may have gone their separate ways with only a greeting sent at Christmas and Diwali, but that's not to say the years have alienated them. Olga took no notice of Paul's lecture. "Giving returns pleasure sevenfold," she said, departing with the clock.

And so it does. Embraced by Asha, who has changed from girl to plump woman, as though liking the fit of prosperity, Olga feels very happy. She adds her outdoor shoes to the line and is conducted inside to be welcomed and introduced. If she cared a jot about such things, she would have to own up to being an oddity, for there is only one other European present—a pale, unhappy-looking girl whose creased white sari looks drab among the Indian women's brilliant silks and heavy jewellery. With pleasure, Olga inhales foreign scents of incense, perfumes, hair-oils and curry powder. She looks about her for the bride and bridegroom. There is Hanu, grown past all recognition, clad in her red wedding sari and with the *tilak* mark set on her forehead. Olga embraces her and gives her the clock. It's true that Hindu custom requires a private opening of gifts to spare embarrassment, but the clock is well and truly exposed since its wetting. Olga dries it on her sleeve, not sorry when a knot of women standing near her gesture and give out approving comments. Olga has given from the heart and, yes, she is glad. Hanu and Kamla are swept off to other arms, and Asha settles Olga on the sofa beside the white girl, who says her name is Rose—

an inappropriate name, thinks Olga, unless it is a wilted specimen. Rose has the air of a chicken huddled on one leg in the rain. She seems to take no interest in the gathering, which stirs Olga to exclaim, making straight her batik skirt, "How remarkable it is! No matter how outward forms differ, the central likeness is there. A wedding is a wedding anywhere; a symbol of hope, of faith in the future. Don't you agree?"

"I used to." Rose lapses into silence. Olga has to draw her story from her piece by piece . . . a sad story, a white girl on holiday, infatuated with a Fiji Indian boy, marrying in spite of joint family opposition, romance fading in a sleazy house in Samabula, a mother-in-law who makes reference constantly and bitterly to the shame and the disgrace of it, the loss of a good match and a good shop through the wiles of white girls who know not even how to cook *roti*.

"Govindalal brought me to Auckland to get us both away. He said his cousins would be pleased to put us up, but they're not cousins at all. They don't like Fiji Indians and they make it plain. And then the police found Govindalal was working, when we came on a visitor's permit, and they deported him. I couldn't go. We didn't have the fare. I'm left here on my own."

Olga is indignant when she sniffs bureaucracy. "Can't your parents help you?" she suggests. Rose smiles her faint, sad smile, and says they live in Melbourne.

Olga shifts uncomfortably, places her gold-thread slippers together, and stares around the room. "Someone's arriving—what are they doing?" She would like to change the subject from Rose and her problems. She has come here to rejoice and now she feels depressed and somehow guilty.

"The Brahmin has come," Rose explains without enthusiasm. "Now the wedding will take place."

Hanu and Kamla, garlanded with flowers, seat themselves on the wedding cloth and the Sanskrit prayers begin. As Olga watches, she sends up her own hopes that things will work out for the young couple. They may be Westernised and allowed choice, but who's to say that improves the odds of success? Men have come and gone in her own life, affecting her little more than waves rippling over sand. Could she have chosen differently? Does it really matter?

The priest binds the hands of the couple together. Before the picture of Krishna and Radha the chants continue. Petals drift into the bowl of fire. Olga thinks, We are symbols, just as they are—by the time the smoke has cleared and historians try to make sense of the present's ashes, it's less what we've felt than what we've done that will be judged.

After the ceremonial giving of gifts and money, there is laughter, and embracing, and food carried in, and plates handed round, and dividings and subdividings within the family groups. Women begin chattering in Hindi. Men edge away to the kitchen where Olga observes a bottle of whisky tucked away behind the Coca Cola. She smiles to herself, takes a glass of sweetened milk and a *papadum,* and dutifully goes back to sit with Rose. In truth, she'd much prefer to mix with the women, eye the gift table, guess at the gossip being exchanged with many gesticulations and expressive laughs. Yet Rose has pricked her conscience; unfairly, for it's not Olga's fault she's white. Rose sits there, picking at saffron rice in a way that makes Olga feel greedy, stuffing herself with *jelabis.*

"Aren't you hungry?" she asks Rose. "Can I fetch you the *puris*? A little cake?"

Rose shakes her head. Her gaze moves from group to group of cheerful Indians and her eyes fill with tears, so pitifully that Olga understands why she has felt such uneasiness.

"I would only like to be with my own kind," whispers Rose. Her tears are really flowing, eroding Olga's willpower so that she is not even surprised, hearing herself invite Rose for a visit, just a little break away. Rose is not surprised either. She accepts, as they both knew would be the case.

Paul's birthday comes and goes, unremarked on.

That wasn't Olga's fault. Paul's like that lately; keeping to himself. She has tried to placate him, saying, "It's only for a very short stay." But Paul seems unimpressed.

Rose has tried to be accommodating, has put her suitcase in the corner and made her bed on the sofa. How can Paul blame her when she swells and scratches, and confesses her allergy to cat fur? What choice had Olga, despite Rose's protestations, except to shift her upstairs into Paul's tower? She packed his clothes neatly into cartons for him. Why did he make such a fuss when he came home from work?—though coping with his idea of fuss leaves Olga at a loss. She'd understand accusations, shouts, a slanging match, but his frozen presence seems designed to make her guilty. Why should she feel guilty? She's doing her best in rather less than ideal circumstances. Paul eats in silence, goes for long walks by himself, sits pointedly on the lumpy sofa until they all begin to feel unwelcome and retire to bed at half past nine.

She thinks he doesn't understand and explains how poor Rose is husbandless, displaced. "When is the money being sent for her fare?" is his response. Olga can see Rose thinks he's heartless, the way she tells him a stranger can't understand the ways of the extended family. Govindalal's entirely in his mother's power. If only

Paul could see that woman, squatting to grind spices, chewing her gums in disgust at the presence of a white girl whose children, should she bear the doubtful fruit of mixed union, will be casteless.

Paul remains unmoved. His cold gaze on Rose's bedraggled chignon and drooping sari upsets Olga more than Rose.

"Suggestions, anyone?" cries Olga, desperately.

"I'd like to go to bed." Paul taps his foot and glares.

Paul turns and tosses half the night.

He hates the way the blankets slide off and the cats purr and tread up and down, kneading their claws so that he swears and kicks at them, and his displacement.

He doesn't care about Rose. He doesn't want to come home to neglect and disorder and dead ash in the grate. He feels his rage, cold and banked up for he can't let it flare against such helpless, passive creatures as Olga's visitors. Instead he hates Olga for letting such a situation come about. Home from work, he stands in the doorway. He takes in the sight of dirty dishes and unset fire. He sees how Kathleen twists her hands and shuts her eyes while Rose continues the saga of her tragic life, lifting her mud-stained hem to pick her feet despondently. Armloads of washing and nesting cats possess his sofa bed—and Lilah, jumping on the springs, shouting at Olga because her costume for the school play should have been made a week ago.

"Where is my dinner?" Paul demands, like a patriarch.

Olga is fiddling about at the stove, stirring something stew-like. She wheezes and reaches for her atomiser, as though begging him to accept the temporary nature of the chaos. But Paul fears Rose. There is a subtle power exercised by victims. He doesn't care that Olga thinks he's hard, cold. Well might she say, Only a short stay, just a little while. Shortness is comparative . . . true in the context of eternity: day by day, unendurable. Olga lugs the stew-pot to the table and summons them to eat.

"In this pigsty?" enquires Paul in disbelief. He turns his back on them and slams the door, but not before he sees how Olga sits and bows her head, and Rose offers her mottled hand in comfort as though to say, *Accept— man is born to sorrow, as the sparks fly upward.*

Paul marches up the road.

It is still daylight. "When the summer comes," he has said to Steffie, "I'll take you flounder-fishing down at Little Muddy. By Christmas, maybe you'll have your bike and we'll go out riding."

But summer is far from his mind. The wind's cold. The bush is disturbed. Like a woman, he thinks— bestride the Manakau's shores, tides tugging at her hem. She's too self-contained to care. He can hear her breathe, sucking in the gusts that try to subdue and penetrate her. Let her toss her head and moan; it's only surface tension. Nature and man can't touch her rule. Neither fear nor love inhabit her. She is a remorseless housewife, maintaining herself by sloughing off the weak. At night he hears the shrill screams and deadwood cracks, her sentence on those that cannot pay. Let the day shine on her surfaces, dimpled, dappled, shot through with light. Let her display her beauty like any woman holding out the lure of restfulness. If ever she cracks apart and yields, it will be in triumph, on her own terms. She has been deemed intact, protected from man, permitted her reserve. Yielding would be her last word, the cataclysm, the crack of doom.

Rose taps on Olga's boudoir door.

"Come in," calls Olga, sitting forward on the chaise longue, then falling back when she sees it's only Rose.

"I am a burden on your household."

"Not for a moment," wheezes Olga, taking up her atomiser.

But Rose explains she's sensitive to atmosphere and Paul's unkind behaviour has affected her. "Ah," she sighs, staring at Julia's treasures, "how much better for us all if I could go back to Govindalal."

Olga agrees that money is a pest.

"At least you have given me a home," acknowledges Rose.

Olga sits up straight again. "Your husband is saving every cent to bring you back to him as soon as possible."

But Rose says Olga does not know the way it is. "He will be off drinking Coca Cola with his friends, forgetting me, his wife. His mother will make mischief to get rid of me."

"If I had the fare," Olga feels pressed to explain, "I would gladly lend it to you, but I don't."

"I could not possibly accept," says Rose. "Already you have been so kind and generous. Who else would bring a stranger into her home or give away so valuable a clock to strangers?"

"Not strangers. Friends. Dear, old friends." It is somehow alarming, seeing how Rose examines the silver-backed brushes, weighing them in her hand like someone making herself comfortable in the face of a necessary and extended visit. Rose nods at her words, agreeing that friendship is indeed a beautiful thing.

Olga is hurt.
Paul won't stay for Marian's demonstration.
"I've baked a sponge-cake. There will be games, prizes. Rowan and Josie are making a special effort to be here..."
"I am a man," states Paul in case Olga has forgotten. "I don't use make-up."
"Neither do I. Soap and water's always done me. But please won't you stay, just for a little while?"
"No," says Paul. The pink house has been invaded by a company of women. Their neediness suffocates him. He feels a strong wish for male company—or, failing that, his own.
"The chairs need shifting and the little table must come up from downstairs."
But Paul just looks at Olga coldly, as though to say, This was your idea to open a sanatorium for the deranged.
"I'm going out. Get Rose to help. I'm taking Steffie for a walk." Olga tries to hide her disappointment. Rose is quickly at her side, pressing her shoulder, her touch agreeing, Ah, women, how we suffer!

Paul strides out and Steffie has to scuttle to keep up.

They pass the dairy and the park. They leave the primary school behind. Still Paul keeps walking at a pace that says, If we were looking for clues, that time's long gone. Today there's no time to peer in tree-holes, search under leaves. There are times to weigh up: times to act decisively.

In the end he slows, as though walking has defused his anger, and Steffie catches up with him. Horses graze the bumpy paddocks. Paul points beyond them to the overcast horizon, stuck with toetoe like candles on a cake.

"That was a Maori fortification once. Can you see them, Steffie? Warriors creeping over that ridge and pouring into the valley? They say there was a battle fought here and that the spirits of the dead still take this route on their journey out to Piha and the western sea." Steffie twists a silver toetoe frond for himself and Paul nods. "Yes, all men were warriors in those days. The boys learned how to stalk and kill. It was expected that the men would lead." He adds, "Of course that was a long time ago."

But Steffie's out of earshot. He comes running back to tug Paul's hand and point out a heron stilt-stepping on a soggy patch of grass. Paul ruffles his hair, because he's tried to understand what Paul likes. "It's found a wet, open space just right for a blue heron. It wouldn't like the bush. See, there are right places for everyone and what's right now might not be, later on. Steffie, I want you to listen because I won't be here for ever. You'd better understand that." Steffie zigzags away from Paul on to the reserve, hurling his toetoe spear. Startled ducks wing high, wrinkling the grubby bedsheet of the sky.

Helen walks past Dennis's garden.

But Dennis doesn't live here any more. He's packed his bags and shifted in with Helen.

It is Saturday and spring, and Helen is on her way to Steffie's home to pay a formal call. She stares at the garden Dennis has deserted, fearing yet hoping for a glimpse of the wife, cast on her knees beside the iris and nemesia beds.

But Marian is not at home. The house looks empty and Helen feels disappointed, as a spy would, and relieved, as a thief might, slipping past unseen.

She checks the number on the box around the corner. Although the letter-box looks new, the house does not. Helen thinks, So this is where Steffie lives. Olga's pink house, roosting up there, is hard to classify. It looks run-down but not despondent. The thicket of trees and tangled grass suggest a secretive retreat—a picture-book hideaway surrounded by a moat. But there is no moat, just the ditch. Helen steps across and slowly starts the upward climb. The environment seems as difficult to pinpoint as Steffie's actual handicap. The psychologist has eliminated any precise, genetic condition. There's nothing relevant in the textbooks. Yet the boy's physical clumsiness, lack of speech, emotional lag seem real enough. He thinks Steffie should experience the pressure of normal peer-group interaction at a normal school. And Helen agrees. She has been looking forward to bringing Olga the good news. Yet somehow, eyeing the pink house, she feels less sure of her welcome there.

Paul checks his watch.

They've completed the long climb to the village and his anger has been drained. "It's too early to go back—their tea-party won't be over. Come on, I'll teach you how to hitch-hike. Stick out your thumb like this." And he smiles at Steffie's expression when a passing car stops as though by magic and they are offered a ride.

"I work here," Paul says, as he and Steffie climb out and start the walk along the muddy track towards the gardens. "When I started there were cabbages, only cabbages. I used to bring them home for tea, remember? But they're all finished now. It's like I said. Right places, right times for everything. Cabbages aren't growing, but something else will. We've been rotary-hoeing. Then we'll plant out. That's why it looks so bare. But you come by in a few months and there'll be new crops growing like billy o."

Steffie likes the market garden. Or the new experience, perhaps. Paul tries to imagine Steffie's world before Paul came—the minibus, the special school, the pink house, and watchful Olga. No wonder brown paddocks set him frisking, weaving in and out of puddles and looking back to check if Paul is watching him.

"That's about it," Paul says after he has shown Steffie the shed, the packing crates, cultivators, fertilizers. "You know where I work now. If I'm not at home I'm most likely here . . . O.K.?"

Steffie nods.

Marian too has been transformed.

Life was humdrum. Now she hardly knows what will happen next. Dennis's decision to leave her has let loose a whole predicament of change.

There is her husband, here today, gone tomorrow.

There is her job, and how organized and determined she has to be to succeed.

There are all the unpredictable events of house-to-house visiting—marriage fights, reconciliations, sad husbands, alcoholics, savage dogs.

And she has coped so well that she has received a letter from the sales manager, promoting her to the next level of the incentive selling scheme and enclosing her lucky ticket. It is deckle-edged and gold-embossed, and the winner will be announced within the month. With the ticket came a luncheon invitation which she accepted. She propped the ticket beside her make-up mirror. She sees it every morning, putting on her face.

Things work out, Marian concludes as she sits by herself in the evening, checking the following day's appointments and balancing her accounts.

When a husband goes off with another woman, one might expect a wife to feel upset. She did at first. Even cried. Now she just feels released. It's as though a sentence of *not guilty* has been passed on her. Resentment, pay-back, they've vanished into thin air the way a soufflé can disappear between the oven and the plate.

Though it's lucky she has the job to make up for losing Dennis.

Olga's friends look like unsuitable candidates for *The Alchemoist Experience.*

Josie and Rowan, Kathleen and Rose aren't really the base material of *femmes fatales.* Rowan slumps withdrawn behind her tangled hair. Kathleen twists the buttons on her blue cardigan and tries to hide in the kitchen. Marian appraises clumping Josie, depressed

Rose, distraught Olga, and she reminds herself how fortunate it is that the training course has fitted her to cater for all comers.

They're not yet ready to enter into the spirit of Marian's demonstration, that much is plain. Despite the efforts Olga has made to set out the good china and display the sponge-cake and the sandwiches, there is about her sitting-room an air of displacement, as though of necessity refugees are gathered who might prefer to be elsewhere. But Marian smiles and claps her hands. She knows exactly what to do to make them all relax.

They must have fun, for that's how sales are made. Her case is crammed with ideas, gifts, prizes. Won't they play? says Marian.

They have no option. She lines up the chairs, pulls out a blindfold and a bell and reaches for the radio.

Games break the ice: and ice is no advantage in this game, feels Marian.

Helen can hear sporadic blasts of music.

There is a clear voice calling out instructions, and the sound of much activity—bumps, clatters, a bell tinkling as though a fight is being refereed.

Going even slower, Helen mounts the shaky steps and peeps through the doorway.

A figure with bandaged eyes huddles near the doorway with a bell. Beside her stands a well-groomed woman in control of a portable radio from which she lets loose intermittent pop music, at the same time explaining to the reluctant figure at her side, "No, no, Kathleen . . . ring the bell *after* the music stops." Around the circle of chairs run figures, perhaps in fancy-dress.

Helen wonders if this is some kind of celebration, although the celebrants do not appear to radiate much joy.

Helen feels relieved that she's picked an inappropriate time to call. She is preparing to go away when Marian glances around and forgets the tussle going on between the wild-looking redhead and the woman in the crumpled sari—who despite her limpness is just now displaying distinct aggression. In fact she wins, fending off the redhead to plant herself firmly on the one remaining chair. Marian ignores her and rushes to claim Helen.

Helen is a godsend. A fitting model for Marian's art has been provided. Helen protests. She only wants a word with Olga and clearly this isn't the time. She will come back . . . she's not a customer . . . in fact, she hardly uses make-up. . . .

Marian reproaches her. Surely she has a boyfriend, an attractive girl like Helen? Women have always used a touch of artifice to win their men. Let Marian just demonstrate and Helen will be most pleasantly surprised.

Helen bows her head and lets Marian lead her to the chair. Colour charts and lotions are brought forth. Marian goes to work, demonstrating the subterfuge of beauty. She works rouge with skilful hands. On Helen's cheek appears a blush.

Paul comes home late with Steffie.

He can only stand and stare. Olga's sitting-room is possessed by a ritual circle, passing potions from hand to hand and performing spells with plastic pots, like witches at a Sunday coven in suburbia.

Olga concludes it's been a dreadful day.

There have been arguments over the sleeping arrangements and fights over Steffie, and Paul and Rose have all but come to blows, and her head does ache. She can't think of cooking dinner, when all she longs for is solitude.

She feels disoriented. A bizarre wind blows through her home. Is madness contagious, like the measles? For it seems to her they're all quite mad . . . that teacher, wanting to shift Steffie to a normal school to bear the brunt of normal children's cruelty . . . and Paul, turning against Olga there in front of everyone, saying she held Steffie back from normal life with her possessiveness. Then Rose said, "He does not understand a mother's love," and Paul turned on her. Rose just murmured, "He is unsympathetic. I felt his coldness from the start."

Paul ordered her to leave, and Rose said, "I have as much right to be here as you. You are just a boarder. Olga has invited me." Olga tried to put things in perspective. "Only for a short stay," she pleaded with them, pressing her forehead. But Paul stared in disgust at Rose as though she tippled on self-pity, and laced her words with gloom.

Now Paul comes back into the room, and Olga can see he's in the kind of mood that makes her suddenly remember her husband, and Angelo. "I've had enough!" he shouts. "It's a madhouse."

"He does not like us," Rose concludes. "He is like the Hindu men who think of us as the Black Mother, Kali, with her matted hair and red-stained palms, the snakes about her feet. They hang a string of skulls round her neck and dead bodies from her ears. That is what they think of women."

"Shut up!" roars Paul, in such a temper Olga hardly recognizes him. Rose says dismissingly, "What do you know of love, cold as you are?" Paul strides from the room, slamming the door so hard the curtains billow and young Olga shivers in her picture-frame.

"What does he know of love?" repeats Rose to Olga; who just places her fingers on her temples and closes her eyes.

TEN

Rowan lays plans with Josie.

Their petition has gone to council, yet the bulldozers work on. Yesterday men demolished the boundary wall and erected a temporary wire fence.

"They're going to do it—destroy those lovely trees," says Josie.

"We should try to stop them." But Rowan sounds half-hearted. The fairness she has always believed in seems tainted. Word is going round the hospital that Jacob, Charge Nurse, has run away with his former patient, Angela. There's no proof—just rumour, with rumour's unpleasant hint of truth.

They evolve a plan of action. Josie says the death of trees is one thing; the murder of several dozen nurses and supporters surely another?

"I suppose Olga and Paul might turn up," says listless Rowan.

"Good. We'll round up our posse and occupy our places by sunrise." And Josie reties her red bandana against the sun.

It's hot beside the lake at Western Springs. Joggers pound past, sweating. Rowan tucks up her skirt and examines her winter pallor with dislike. "I might get my hair streaked," she says without conviction. Josie, trying to absorb an early tan, wriggles her jean legs as high as she can. "Hideous, isn't it?" She fingers the zipper-like scar which runs from knee to ankle.

"Do you ever hate your mother, Josie?"

"Half the time," says cheerful Josie.

"I just hate Olga sometimes."

"Was she hard on you as a child?"

"She was very kind. That's the trouble. She makes me feel guilty for hating her."

"Try standing up to her." Josie laughs, but Rowan is not amused. Swans drift on the lake, peaceful gondolas, cygnets riding their gentle wake. They'll shed their baby down soon and swim away, and the parents will let them go without clinging.

Rowan sighs. "I'm not sure I trust them, do you?"

"I envy them. They're elegant." Josie tosses bread scraps as more birds gather near the shore.

"They scared me when I was small," remembers Rowan.

"Why hate your mother? What's happened?"

"Take the way she invited us home, then expected us to sleep on the floor like kids."

"*I* didn't object. I thought it was fun. Imagine creeping in with Paul in the middle of the night."

But Rowan won't see the funny side of things. It was always the way; going to Olga for support, finding her bed given away again to strangers.

"*And* she borrows and doesn't pay me back."

"Then say No."

But it's not that simple. Rowan rolls on her stomach, thinking Josie's not the sensitive nurse she used to be. She combs her fingers through the grass. "I think I *will* get my hair streaked," she decides.

Paul feels calm.

Peace has come down. Kathleen has withdrawn to the basement and Rose to the tower. The children are in bed, and Olga in her boudoir. The old gramophone sends faint music through the wall—Olga's loneliness pleading with him. He prefers to be alone. It has always been that way. As long ago as he can remember, people have found his solitariness puzzling, as though humans are meant to live in litters like newborn dependents. Being on your own is suspect. His mother thought so, and his teachers.

Playing round graves! Surely there's a friend you'd like to invite for the weekend?

Though Paul's exam results are satisfactory, he needs to improve his social skills and build his team spirit.

If he was born that way, why expect change now? If needs are great, expectations high, that might point to more than a single man can achieve. But he has modest hopes. He doesn't make idle promises or wear his heart on his sleeve. People like Rose call him self-centred. True—he is in search of the calm centre within himself; trying to take responsibility for his own peace of mind.

Rose calls him cold, unfeeling. That's not true. He may not dive in to passionate relationships, but love's come surprisingly in this unlikely household. Love's stolen up on him and made him grow. Now its claims bind him hand and foot.

Kali, the female goddess, has four arms. She is wily and she presents her claims submissively, as victims can. But need is not love. When, in the name of need, possessiveness steps in, it's up to the one claimed to make his stand or be undermined. Long ago, a random event carried off Paul's father and brought his first lesson in the claims of love.

Safe in the arms of Jesus.
You will have to stay with me and take care of me, Paul.
I need you, now your father's gone.

And he did. It seemed his duty.
You're such a comfort to your mother, not many sons are like you.

And when at last she died, he discovered the feel of freedom, and he cherished it.

The soulful aria directs him to listen and pay heed. Disembodied notes of sorrow at the pain of parting seep through the wall cavities and door cracks. The room turns its claims on him—Steffie's spear, Lilah's schoolbooks, Rose's cardigan, Olga's image challenging him from the picture-frame. Only Kathleen's slipped away, leaving nothing.

Paul's things are there too, stacked in the corner in boxes. He doesn't own much—clothes, typewriter, books. He goes to the kitchen for twine and fashions a carrying handle and tests the weight of his parcel of essentials.

He knocks on Olga's door. She calls and he goes in.

She is reclining on the chaise longue, the curtains drawn, the lamp lit, its light tender on the faded carpet and glowing in the wood grain and leaping, like fish from a shadowed pool, from the silver brushes on the dressing table. Olga's white nightdress is too long, it trails down to the floor as she lies back, reading, a dictionary open beside her. Her lips move, testing the accent of her French. Though Paul has hurt her and accused her of the very worst failings, possessiveness and disregard for others' freedom, she looks him in the eye. Olga cannot read any apology there and she looks down at her book.

"*'Dans le Labyrinthe'*—Robbe-Grillet. Such gloomy stuff. These novelists, I sometimes wonder if they ever live a life at all."

"I'm leaving, Olga."

"*Saccadé?*" Olga murmurs, consulting the dictionary, "*le bruit saccadé* . . . jerking? the jerky noise?"

"I said I'm going." He knows she can hear him, although the aria is very loud, coming to its climax.

". . . *le bruit saccadé des talons ferres sur l'asphalte* . . . Abrupt? Yes, 'the abrupt noise of heels tapping on the pavement.' "

"I'll pick up my books later." Paul waits. Olga keeps reading. He turns away and closes the door behind him.

The record finishes quite soon and Olga doesn't renew it. Silence flows over her. She swings her feet to the floor. Holding her nightdress bunched so she doesn't trip, she crosses to the door and looks along the passage to the sitting-room. The light is off. She switches it on and checks that room, then the kitchen. She looks in the children's rooms and then in the bathroom. Olga returns to her boudoir.

Let him go or stay, that is the way she looks on it.

It's not her way to beg and plead with anyone.

She picks up her book. It has fallen shut and she has lost her place. She reads out loud from the beginning again. " *Je suis seul ici, maintenant, bien à l'abri. Dehòrs il pleut, dehors on marche sous la pluie en courbant la tête, s'abritant les yeux d'une main tout en regardant quand même devant soi, quelque mètres d'asphalte mouillé; dehors il fait froid, le vent souffle entre les branches noires denudees; le vent souffle dans les feuilles, entrâinant les rameaux entiers dans un balancement, balancement...'"*

It is useless. Her concentration has gone, a sense of pain is invading her.

Marian scans the menu at the Hotel Intercontinental.

She feels entirely at home, as though she eats as a matter of course at restaurants where even the ice has a hand-cut sparkle; as though life in the city backwaters with Dennis was the mis-appointment. Raising her eyes from the menu she smiles, a full, eventful smile, at Hammond Gander, Sales Executive. Hammond and the winner of the *Alchemoist* bonus draw will fly together and first-class on a tour of overseas offices. Developmental training will be offered to the chosen candidate. Hammond likes the look of Marian in red dress and the *Strawberry Ice* collection.

"Do you believe in luck?" he wonders.

Marian's gaze meets his head-on. "I'm not a gambler," she says firmly. "It all boils down to going after what you want."

Hammond relaxes. Marian may be a recent and relatively inexperienced recruit but she says what's on her mind. And that frees him to be direct. He runs through a few of the finer points of the accompanied tour. Marian doesn't blink a shadowed eye. Instead she leans towards him, letting her *Crushed Strawberry* fingertips fall lightly on the mohair of his jacket sleeve.

"Who picks the marble?" It is her turn to speculate.
"I do," confirms Hammond.
They smile across the table.

Olga doesn't like the new Rowan who comes home for a visit.

Rowan's hair is cut very short and tipped with orange lights. Her facial bones stand out, somehow naked-looking, and she wears new clothes Olga thinks are vulgar. The trousers are too tight and the neckline too low-cut. As for her shoes . . . the kind that self-assertive madams prance on, pushing past Olga in the city. "I only hope your eyebrows grow back," says Olga.

All the same, it's good to have her daughter home. Rowan's always been her comfort when times were hard and money short. How the bills are mounting up! There's been another mix-up over the benefit payments, which she hasn't had the energy to argue out with Social Welfare yet. Paul has removed more than his presence. Olga finds the lack of income very awkward when she dares to think about it.

She asks Rowan if she can borrow, just a bit to tide her over. Rowan raises the pencil-lines which serve as eyebrows and says No. Olga tries to make the points Rowan must have missed. They haven't a sou. The cupboards are bare. Olga is ill. Paul has deserted them.

Rowan says she's sorry, but she's several bills in debt herself. Olga starts to wheeze. She opens the fridge to prove she speaks the truth. Next they will all be eating the weeds from the roadside. Rowan is unmoved. Olga can scarcely believe how hard her gentle daughter has become.

Rowan takes tea in uncomfortable silence. She has heard these stories many times. She knows she must not listen or her roots, just forming in the brittle grip of independence, will snap. She will collapse, a gust of Olga's insinuating guilt will blow her clean away. She realises that for her own sake she must leave.

Yet Olga looks so small and lonely sitting there, stirring her tea round and round. Rowan could even forget her resolution and open up her purse, but Olga wheezes suddenly, "It was always the way, ingratitude has divided parents and children from time immemorial."

Rowan collects her bag and stands up. "I'm leaving now, mother," she says. "Don't forget about the demonstration. And if you're hard-up, sell something."

Her spiked heels take her away. Olga sits by herself, feeling this desert.

Olga slops meat loaf into a rusty baking tin.

She stands despondent at the sink. She has the house to herself. The children are at school, Kathleen has returned to her cottage at the beach, Rose has departed. Olga felt guilty, asking her to move out. Yet she did it and she stuck to it, despite the tragic consequences Rose predicted for herself. And when Olga found Rose had equipped herself against emergency with Julia's silver brushes, her guilt evaporated.

She should set up her easel and start to paint again. Creativity once meant so much to her. Her talent might be limited, yet she felt alive, fulfilled. When he went away, Paul took more than just a handy male figurehead from the household. Lilah's been behaving badly, and

Steffie mopes by the window and won't even walk with Olga to the dairy. Olga feels his absence herself. Oh, she can't put a precise definition on her feelings. They all loved Paul, but in such a simple way she'd hardly noticed until he left.

She remembers standing at the bench once, making soup. Paul was hammering away, working on his letter-box. The first one fell to bits but he kept at it, and in the end the result was splendid. He called her to admire his handiwork. Then he hugged her and said she had the gift of faith in people—look at what her praise had made of him, a carpenter.

She left him sanding the box and went back to her kitchen. The sunlight streamed across the chopping-board so that in the pumpkin slice she seemed to see a sunrise, and in the crumpled silverbeet a mountain-range, and at the carrot's heart a sunburst, and in the onion flesh a pearl. Now when she looks there are only old vegetable choppings and a dirty window-glass.

Olga wanders outside with a crust of bread for the sparrows. The garden looks more overgrown than ever. Spring declares itself everywhere. That creeping press of greenery, that fertile thrust of life, it makes her tired somehow.

Rowan and Josie are sitting in the magnolia trees.

A few creamy cups stand above the leathery leaves. Their season for flowering is almost over and Rowan feels like crying. It doesn't seem fair that people can kill such an old and patient rejoicing. She does feel like crying, often. Exam. nerves and tiredness, Josie says. They're likely reasons, though rumour has more to do with it.

Rowan and Josie, from their bird's eye view, watch workmen dismantle the temporary fence and move the bulldozer into the garden. Trucks disturb yellow dust-clouds which drift towards the trees.

"Geneva Willett tried to do herself in last night. She cut her throat in the linen closet," calls Josie from the other tree. "The night staff found her, gore from head to foot and all over the sheets."

Rowan imagines Geneva, a patient she has never met, one who has probably spent most of her life in hospital. In that confined environment she has eaten, slept, bathed, made friends; perhaps loved people who may or may not have returned her love. Not so different from Rowan's own experience. Who can say, Geneva Willett might have sat under the magnolia tree, dreaming of someone she yearned to be loved by.

She wants to die, if Josie's tale is true. Rowan's not thought much about death—some people might have nothing left if their dreams are taken from them.

Olga hasn't come. She wouldn't, without Paul. Though anyone could see he wouldn't stay for ever, his leaving has hit Olga hard. Maybe she loved him? Olga with a private world of needs, illusion? You don't expect mothers to have them.

I could tell Olga about Jacob, she thinks.

Josie shouts something but it's impossible to have a conversation across the space. Now and then an orderly or gardener walks near the trees and calls out encouragement. There were pages and pages of signatures when the petition went off—and now only Josie and Rowan sitting in the trees. People are unpredictable. Olga and Paul would have come, if they'd still been together. Despite their differences they believed in the same things.

The wind freshens and Rowan shivers. The tree replies with small creaks and groans, as though it knows death is near. One of the men approaches across the green lawn. He speaks to the girls reasonably enough. Rowan can't hate him but Josie is less sensitive.

"Fuck off!" she yells when he asks politely if they won't come down and let the work proceed. He explains he has a job to do; that the trees are old, they've had their day. "Would you like someone to say that about you?" shouts Josie. "When you're redundant and peeing yourself in some old man's home, I hope you remember today. Trees have as much right to life as you." Patiently he advises that she must come down or be removed by force. Josie responds by throwing an Olde Stoney can at him. It glances off his ear, splashing him with ginger-beer.

"You could have knocked him out." Rowan feels embarrassed. It has always been her problem to see the other person's point of view.

"It was nearly empty." Josie clings to the tree fork protectively.

Trucks approach. They park near Rowan's tree. She's only been up there a matter of hours. Why should she feel she's been making her stand for a lifetime against some mastering will, which only now, at one p.m., personifies as several cheery workmen carrying chain-saws and axes, coming towards her across the placid sward? Rowan's armpits grow damp and itchy, and her bladder insistent.

"Coming down, darling?" calls a blue-overalled fellow with freckles and a friendly grin.

Rowan realises she's ready. Sitting in the trees has been her statement; like any statement, made now, done with. But Josie is preparing for battle, signalling her to climb higher. Rowan stays where she is. They bring a ladder. The friendly council worker climbs up, eye-level; Josie would give him a boot in the face, thinks Rowan as she gathers her duffle bag of supplies and climbs down. Her legs are trembling. For a self-conscious moment she fears her bladder might betray her there in front of all the men. Josie is still aloft and Rowan looks up, afraid abuse and cans might rain on her head, too, but Josie is preoccupied with climbing higher, her broad backside framed by the magnolia leaves. Rowan crosses the grass alone. She feels ashamed to have let Josie down and relieved she has followed her own instincts and given in. Josie's a fighter, a champion of causes; they will seek her out. But in the tree, as she thought about Jacob and herself, Paul and Olga, Rowan saw there were some things that had to be accepted. Now she feels calm, though Josie might say she was weak, as she walks away from the trees.

Behind her she can hear the chain-saws, ripping into the branches. Josie stays in her tree while they trim the branches around her and drown her abuse in the roar of machinery. At last she comes down, white and exhausted-looking, and goes back to the Nurses' Home.

Olga sits with her sketch-pad in the park.

Quietly she contemplates the near scene of lawns, paths, seats, swings. Roads' boundaries edge two sides of the park. Willows, gums and bamboo form its other perimeters. Beyond those, native bush mounts tier on tier, its colours old and sombre greens lightened with tree fern and growing tips. Olga will have to memorise and mix those greens, and the exhausted blue of the sky. Ragged ranges fringe its emptiness. The clouds seem to shred and disintegrate like old curtains at the rough tug of the wind.

Cold up there. Those cirrus are always the sign.

Cold in the park, though it's only mid-afternoon. The guarding ranges intercept the sun and Olga shivers.

A mother rocks her toddler on the swing, then wanders towards the store. An Alsatian comes bounding and the clamour of gulls rise as they perch, jeering, on the restroom roof. A chain reaction of frustrated barks bounces off the hills. The dog turns and gallops off. Olga eyes the blank page. There is a scene she might sketch, but it is not what she is looking for. If she dives in without seeing, all she will end up with is a picture made of lumps of paint. She can't think how anyone might paint a dog's bark, a mother's care, a mountain's age. She draws without heart and soon puts the pencil down. Forcing herself on the page will not work.

The sun slinks below the tree-tops. Furtive shadows encroach upon the grass and Olga, sitting there. A school bus passes by—then school's out and Lilah and Steffie will want their dinner soon. Food—she must see to that. Weeks since the benefit arrived, and she hasn't had the energy to face the city and officialdom. It's happened before, it always gets sorted out eventually. She used to be more philosophical when food ran out and money wasn't there. Or is she only saying that? Was life always an endurance of loneliness and lack?

Olga feels dizzy. Apart from a few barley sugars she unearthed from her bag, she hasn't had a thing to eat all day, nor yesterday. The dairy would let her buy on tick but she won't ask for herself. The children must eat though. She will send Lilah with a note. Olga turns her attention back to the park. If she can be patient she feels she will understand something that at present escapes her. It is something she needs to know and it will not be hurried and that is that. She inspects the scene again. Though it's hardly four o'clock the moon is rising, pallid, as though the effort of being in that bled atmosphere has taken any power it might have to affect the earth.

She knows the feeling well. Like the moon she must obey and do what's given her to do, but she feels washed-out, winter has sapped her, Paul's going has sapped her, she can hardly bother going on. Here she is under a dying sky, a dead moon up there and Olga fading, going out. Her eyes are tired. She does not fight.

Boys ride pell-mell in the park, whiling away the little that remains of the day.

They notice Olga sleeping on the grass near the toilets. A few laugh. Most pay no attention. The ways of grown-ups—who knows, who cares? When they are going home for dinner and see she still sleeps on, one boy remembers and mentions to his mother that a lady in the park won't wake up. The matter is investigated, an ambulance is summoned and Olga is taken away to hospital.

Lilah feels uneasy.

Funny, Olga not home and the light fading; the house just theirs, and the hungry cats'. She says firmly to Steffie, "It's only a minor catastrophe, Olga will be home soon. You keep watch and I'll cook dinner." And although they both sense Olga won't appear on the track, her kit stuffed with groceries, Steffie watches while Lilah goes to the kitchen. The cats spring off the bench where they have been nosing into empty tins and push anxiously against her ankles. Lilah searches the fridge and cupboards. She finds bread crusts and smears them with yeast extract, and makes two cups of cocoa. She carries dinner to the porch. Without milk, the cocoa isn't nice but they drink it.

Lilah switches on the radio and starts her homework. She lets Steffie use her felt-tips for a treat. With the sound of music in the background they work side by side as though Olga's there in her boudoir, playing the gramophone. Lilah reads Steffie a story at bedtime. Steffie sits close, not listening. Lilah keeps on reading. The sound of her voice keeps the dark outside. "We'll leave on all the lights," she says, "so Olga can see when she comes in the night."

Steffie wakes at dawn.

He peeps into Olga's boudoir and checks the other rooms. Quietly, then, he leaves the house. Going in his jerky, crab-like way, he turns right at the main road and follows the route Paul showed him. Remembering the hitch-hiking lesson he sticks out his thumb. A bread van picks him up. Soon he's outside Paul's shed. Paul doesn't seem to hear the knocking or the noise as Steffie shifts a crate to climb on. Steffie can see him asleep, and bangs on the windowpane. Paul doesn't even respond to that. Steffie has to bang again several times, and call out, "Paul?"

Paul goes back to the house with Steffie.

He cross-questions Lilah, makes necessary phone calls until Olga is located, and tells the children what has happened. The ward sister said Olga was found in a park, on the verge of a diabetic coma, with nothing on her person to identify her. She will have to stay in hospital until she is stabilised, but visitors are most welcome. Paul promises to come.

He walks from room to room. Mounds of dirty washing, barren cupboard, cat messes in the corners all face him with inevitable messages. The cats have changed to scrawny creatures with staring coats. One has littered on a pile of clothes. The still-blind kittens mouth and struggle at their mother's hollow sides. Paul sends Lilah to the shop for supplies. When he brings the platter of meat the cat springs, ravenous, offspring swinging like parasites from her empty teats. There's pleasure in this power of his to deal with practical problems quietly and methodically; he sees her satisfied, lazily stretched out on the washing, kittens in orderly ranks beside her. He bends and scratches behind her ear. She blinks, a languorous flicker. Lilah and Steffie have missed him, it's obvious. And he's missed them. The air of desolation and neglect disturbs him. It wasn't right, walking out on them like that. Leaving is one thing; finding a right way and time is another. He has no choice, at present, except to stay. Hugging Steffie and Lilah, Paul corrects himself. For now, he chooses to stay.

Olga in white hospital gown lies against white pillows.

An intravenous set connects her hand to the bottle hooked above her bed. Her free hand takes Paul's and presses it.

"Paul," she says softly.

"I'm sorry you're sick. How are you?"

"It's a pre-diabetic state or somesuch. I'm on the mend. It's nothing serious."

"Of course it's serious." He still holds her hand. How subdued and frail she looks, yet she smiles with a hint of her old spirit.

"A minor catastrophe. They say I must eat more particularly and stick to a diet. You should see it—far more than I need. I'll be a mountain. You know, this illness is a godsend. They wait on me like a queen."

"I'd like to come back for a few months to get things in order," says Paul, and Olga sighs and releases his hand as though some tension has gone. "It won't be for ever, Olga."

"Nothing is, Paul."

He thinks she looks happy. Yet some inner doubt changes her expression.

"What's the matter?" he asks. Olga sounds sad as she says, "We needed you and depended on you, Paul. You've made us feel secure. I feel guilty now, you see. What have I given you?"

"You've given me joy." Suddenly he feels it and bends and hugs her so hard the needle in her vein dislodges and they have to summon a nurse to summon a doctor to reinsert the drip. Olga tells everyone she is very sorry for her impetuous behaviour. "My mother used to say, 'Fools rush in where angels fear to tread, and Olga is no angel'." She gestures in a royal way to her audience. "To join the holy company it seems I've still a way to go."

Rowan paints her nails with *Frosted Strawberry Ice*.

"Will I go home for Christmas or not?" she wonders. "Olga's been sick. She probably expects me."

"I'm rostered for duty on Christmas day," Josie says. "I'll swap if you want to work."

"I don't want to hurt her."

"Mmmm."

"I've got to make the break sometime."

"Mmmm."

"Christmas in the Nurses' Home sounds boring."

"Go on, swap."

"Peaceful though. Olga couldn't push her problems on to me."

"You're saying she depends on you and you're scared you still depend on her?"

"What I'm *saying*," Rowan contradicts, in a tone that suggests Josie should save her counselling techniques for her patients, "is, I'm going home for Christmas."

"At least I'll earn penalty rates." Josie wiggles her toes to make the polish dry.

Paul and Helen meet in the bicycle shop.

"What brings you here?" he enquires.

"We're buying a bicycle for Dinah." A salesman is demonstrating the use of outriggers to Dennis.

"Steffie's choosing one too." They watch him spin pedals, stare in mirrors, touch gold and red paintwork. "No hurry, Steffie; take your time."

"What happened? He's come right out of his shell, these last weeks."

Her analogy is appropriate, thinks Paul. He wanted to instruct Steffie to come forth—to crack him open like a seed. But Steffie did it by himself in his own way and time. Paul doesn't share his thoughts with Helen. He isn't given to confiding at shop counters.

"I'm happy he's going to a new school next year. I'll miss him though, you get involved," she adds.

"You do." Paul agrees. "Ready, Steffie? It looks your size."

Paul steers Steffie on a trial run, then does a turn or two around the yard himself. "We'll buy it," he confirms.

Olga sits with Rowan in the shade, her new sketchbook open on her lap. It's Christmas, and they've come to the park to try out the presents—the bicycle, and Lilah's skates. Lilah skims along the concrete path, too absorbed to notice Olga's wave. Olga looks after her, and adds a few lines to the sketch. "What a Christmas!" she exclaims to Rowan. "Steffie's bike, the skates, this book . . . Paul's gone overboard."

"When does he leave?"

"Next month. He's paid for his tickets."

"Won't you miss him very much?"

"Travel will be good for him," says Olga firmly.

"Are you taking proper care of yourself?"

"Like an heirloom!"

Steffie dismounts. He's ridden round and round the park, the red and gold bicycle glittering. Now he hands it over to Paul and starts swinging. Paul slow-pedals towards Rowan. "Have a turn," he offers, dismounting.

"I feel silly. I'm nineteen and I can't even ride a bike."

"Tolstoy was sixty-seven when he learned. Hop on!"

Rowan hitches at her jeans and kicks off her shoes. "Well . . ."

"Don't think about it. Push off and pedal."

Olga watches the bicycle wobble away across the grass.

Natural to be afraid. Anyone would be, faced with the unknown. All the same, Rowan's picking up speed; Paul is having to run to stay with her.

She sees them reach the fringe of the park and allows her gaze to follow the tree line as it climbs towards the sky. Up there, a solitary bird labours. Bobbing and dipping, it presses forward, sketching its path across the vastness. So insignificant it is, Olga can't tell at what point or second it disappears or where it has gone. In all its puniness it was life, though. Now only the inscrutable vacuum confronts her and she sighs. That blue, she will never capture it. It has no personal dimension.

She turns her attention back to the park. The swing creaks rhythmically, as it did before. Rowan is still pedalling, Paul running, Lilah skating on the path, yet the scene has subtly altered. Momentum has destroyed the half-grasped picture. She'll have to begin again. Shifting her vantage point, Olga sits and studies Steffie. As the swing flies high and higher she analyses the way his body leans and his elbows work like levers. She picks up her sketchbook and starts to draw.

THE FRINGE OF HEAVEN

Designed by Barbara Holdridge

Composed in ITC Garamond Light typeface by BG Composition, Baltimore, Maryland

Text printed on 55-pound Glatfelter Supple Offset by Maple Press Company, York, Pennsylvania

Bound in Joanna Devon Cinnamon and Permalin Fern, Burnished Leather Grain, with Multicolor Antique Tropic Blue endpapers, by Maple Press Company, York, Pennsylvania

Jackets printed by Keith Press, Knoxville, Tennessee